THE BLANK WALL

Persephone Book N° 42
Published by Persephone Books Ltd 2003

Reprinted 2009

First published 1947 by Simon & Schuster

Endpapers taken from a late 1940s furnishing fabric
manufactured and sold in the United States,
in a private collection

Typeset in ITC Baskerville by Keystroke

Printed and bound by GGP Media GmbH
on Munken Premium (FSC approved)

ISBN 9781903155325

Persephone Books Ltd
59 Lamb's Conduit Street
London WCIN 3NB
020 7242 9292

www.persephonebooks.co.uk

THE BLANK WALL

by

ELISABETH SANXAY HOLDING

****

PERSEPHONE BOOKS
LONDON

PUBLISHER'S NOTE

****

In 1950 Raymond Chandler wrote to his English publisher, Hamish Hamilton:

> Does anybody in England publish Elisabeth Sanxay Holding? For my money she's the top suspense writer of them all. She doesn't pour it on and make you feel irritated. Her characters are wonderful; and she has a sort of inner calm which I find very attractive. I recommend for your attention, if you have not read them, *Net of Cobwebs*, *The Innocent Mrs Duff*, *The Blank Wall.*

The first of these was published, seven years after its American publication, in 1952 in Britain, and four of the 1930s novels had been published in the UK at the time; otherwise Elisabeth Sanxay Holding vanished on this side of the Atlantic and all-but vanished on the other.

Yet in 1928 *The New York Times* had written about the last of her half-dozen romantic novels, *The Silk Purse*:

> She has managed to make every one of her characters, however unimportant, important. They are as real a

****

> collection of people as ever said yes when they wished to heaven they could say no. Like real people, they talk when they should be silent, are silent when they should say something, and, with the best intentions in the world, quietly wreck each other's lives.

A review like this made it a natural progression for Elisabeth Sanxay Holding to turn from romance to suspense, she herself, or her publisher, having realised that her acute psychological perception should not be wasted on light fiction and that (an important consideration after the stock market crash of 1929) she would make more money from it. Thus she started on a career that turned her into an 'an important precursor to later writers such as Patricia Highsmith and Ruth Rendell', a comment made by Maxim Jakubowski in the *Guardian* in December 2001, the month that *The Deep End*, the 2001 film based on *The Blank Wall*, starring Tilda Swinton, was released. The book was also filmed by Max Ophuls as *The Reckless Moment* in 1949, starring James Mason and Joan Bennett.

Alas, it says a great deal about the publicity given to the cinema, and the difficulty of getting attention for literature that is no longer 'new', that so much has been written about both films but so little about the book on which the screenplays were so closely based. Yet, upon first publication in 1947, *The Blank Wall* was highly praised by American newspapers and magazines; for example, *The New Yorker* 'highly recommended . . . this suspense story with a rare and desirable down-to-earth quality in which a suburban matron, harassed by wartime domestic problems – her husband is overseas –

****

finds herself implicated in the murder of her young daughter's extremely unattractive beau.'

The Blank Wall remains the best of Elisabeth Sanxay Holding's novels and was certainly considered as such by Alfred Hitchcock, who reprinted it in its entirety in his 1959 anthology *My Favourites in Suspense*, along with twenty short stories by writers such as HG Wells and Daphne du Maurier. Hitchcock's view was echoed by the *Herald Tribune* reviewer of the anthology, James Sandoe, who singled out for special praise *The Blank Wall* 'by that astonishing artist, the late Elisabeth Sanxay Holding, whose evocation of nightmare was and still is unique, as reprint publishers might recall to their benefit.' Yet none of them did care to recall it, nor did they in 1981 when Raymond Chandler's letters appeared in print and his 1950 plea to Hamish Hamilton was first published. So Maxim Jakubowski too ended his *Guardian* piece by observing that Hamish Hamilton had declined to take up Raymond Chandler's challenge and that 'maybe the time has come for another publisher to resurrect the exemplary books of Elisabeth Sanxay Holding?' Persephone Books is delighted to be the one to be doing so.

THE BLANK WALL

Chapter One

Lucia Holley wrote every night to her husband, who was somewhere in the Pacific. They were very dull letters, as she knew; they gave Commander Holley a picture of a life placid and sunny as a little mountain lake.

"Dear Tom," she wrote. "It is pouring rain tonight."

She crossed it out, and sat for a moment looking at the window where the rain slid down the glass in a silvery torrent. There's no use telling him that, she thought. It might sound rather dreary. "The crocuses are just up," she wrote, and stopped again. The crocuses are up again for the third spring without you to see them. And your daughter, your idolized little Bee, has grown up without you. Tom, I need you. Tom, I'm frightened.

It was one of her small deceptions to pretend that she had lost her taste for smoking. Cigarettes were very hard to get. It was difficult to keep her father supplied. She would sit by while he smoked, and refuse to join him. No, thanks, Father, I really don't seem to care for them any more.

Yet, hidden in her own room, she always kept a few cigarettes, for special moments. She got one out now and lit it, leaning back in her chair, a tall woman, slight, almost thin, very young looking for her thirty-eight years, with a dark, serious face, and beautiful dark eyes. A pretty woman, if you thought about it, but she herself had almost forgotten that, had lost any coquetry she had ever had.

The house was very quiet this rainy night. Her son David had gone to bed early; old Mr. Harper, her father, was reading in the sitting room. Sibyl, the maid, had stopped creaking about in the room overhead.

Bee was shut in her own room, rebellious, furious; perhaps she was crying. I'm not handling this properly, Lucia Holley thought. If only I were one of those wise, humorous, tolerant mothers in plays and books. But I haven't been wise about this and I'm not tolerant about the man. I hate him.

If Tom were here, she thought, he'd get rid of that beast. If David were older . . . Or if Father were younger . . . But there's nobody. I've got to handle it alone. And I'm doing it badly.

She remembered, with a heart like lead, the visit to New York, to the dingy little midtown hotel where Ted Darby lived. She remembered how she had felt, and how she had looked standing at the desk, asking the pale and supercilious clerk to tell Mr. Darby there was a lady here to see him. Countrified, in her old tweed coat, gray cotton gloves, and round felt hat, she was already at a disadvantage. She did not even look like the wise, humorous, woman-of-the-world mother she so wished to be.

"Mr. Darby'll be right down," said the clerk.

She had sat down on a bench covered with green plush, and waited and waited, in the gloomy little lobby. Presently, as the doorman in uniform sat down beside her, she realized that the bench was for him and his colleagues. He was quite an elderly man, and she thought it might hurt his feelings if she got up and went away too quickly, so that she was still sitting there beside him when Ted Darby came out of the other elevator.

He had come straight toward her, holding out his hand.

"You must be Bee's mother," he had said.

She had taken his hand and that was a mistake. Only, she had never yet refused an outstretched hand; she had acted before thinking.

"Suppose we go into the cocktail lounge?" he had suggested. "It's quiet in there, this time of day."

It was a very small room, dimly lit, smelling of beer and varnish. They had sat at a table in a corner, and after one quick and apprehensive look at him, she had been silent. He was so much worse than she had expected, blond, thin, with an amused smile. Puny, she had thought, and dressed with a sort of theatrical nonchalance, in a powder-blue coat, darker blue flannels, and suède moccasins.

She had refused a drink, and he had ordered a rye for himself, and this had given him another advantage over her. He had been easy and relaxed and she had been in misery.

"I don't want my daughter to see you again, Mr. Darby," she had said, at last.

"My dear lady, isn't that for Bee to decide?" he had asked.

"No," Lucia had said. "She's only a child. Only seventeen."

"She'll be eighteen next month, I believe."

"That doesn't matter, Mr. Darby. If you don't stop seeing Beatrice, I'll have to put this in my lawyer's hands."

"But put what, dear lady?"

"I understand that you're married," she had said.

"But, my dear lady," he said laughing, "what will your lawyer do about that? After all, it's not a crime."

"It's altogether wrong for you to see Beatrice."

"Well, really . . ." he protested. "The poor kid tells me her life is miserably dull. She likes to get around, meet interesting people, and I'm very happy to take her around. She knows I'm getting a divorce, but she doesn't think that's any reason for refusing to see me."

Her visit had been not only utterly useless, but harmful. Ted had told Bee about it and she had been bitterly angry.

"Ted's so good-natured that he only laughed," she had told her mother. "But it doesn't make me laugh. It's the most humiliating, horrible thing that ever happened to me."

"Bee," Lucia had said, "unless you promise not to see him again, you'll have to stop going to art school."

"I *won't* stop going, and I *won't* promise."

"Bee," Lucia said, "Bee, darling, why won't you trust me? I'm only thinking of what's best for you."

"Why don't *you* trust *me?*" Bee had cried. "Ted's the most interesting person I've ever met. He knows all sorts of people, artists, and actors, all sorts of people. I'm *not* having a nasty love affair with him."

"I know you're not," Lucia had said. "But, Bee, you must believe me. Bee—he's not the right sort of man for you to know."

"Well, I *don't* believe you," Bee had said. "You think you know, but you're just terribly old-fashioned. You couldn't possibly understand anyone like Ted."

Then Lucia Holley had used her last weapon, with heavy reluctance.

"Bee, if you don't promise me not to see him, I shan't give you any carfare, any allowance at all."

"You *couldn't* do that!" Bee had cried.

"There's nothing I wouldn't do, to stop this thing," Lucia replied.

She meant that. A week ago, her cousin Vera Ridgewood had telephoned her.

"Lucia, angel, I wonder if you know that your precious child is playing around with a *quite* sinister-looking character. I've seen them *twice* in Marino's bar together and today I saw them going into a place on Madison Avenue."

It doesn't mean anything, Lucia had thought, and she had spoken to Bee about it with very little anxiety.

"Bee, dear, is there someone in the art school you go to bars with?"

"That's Ted Darby," Bee had answered. "He doesn't go to art school. He's in the theatrical business."

"I'd rather you didn't go in bars with anyone, Bee."

"I never take anything but ginger ale."

"But I don't like you going to bars, dear. You could go to a drugstore with this boy."

"He isn't a boy," Bee had said. "He's thirty-five."

Lucia had been anxious now.

"Ask him out here, Bee," she had said.

"I wouldn't ask him under false pretenses," Bee had said. "He wouldn't come like that, either. We talked about it, and I told him that if you knew he was married, you'd never let him set foot in the house."

I didn't say the right things to her, Lucia thought, watching the rain against the window. I've made so many mistakes with Bee, even when she was a little girl. I've objected to her friends. I've been upset when she changed her mind about things. I've done so much better with David. If Tom was here, he'd know just what to say to Bee. Here, now, Duckling . . . ! She did use to look like a little yellow duckling, all ruffled . . .

She got up, and went over to the window, restless and heavyhearted. The rain was streaming down the glass, glittering, with an oily look, the trees swayed a little. At the end of the path stood the queer long shape of the boathouse and beyond that lay the invisible water.

It's too lonely here, she thought. It was a mistake to come here. There aren't enough young people. David doesn't much care, but if Bee had met some nice boys, perhaps this wouldn't have happened. Perhaps.

There was someone in the boathouse. She saw a little flame spring out and slant sidewise and die. She saw another one that was steady for an instant. Someone was striking matches in there. A tramp? she thought. A drunken man, who'll set fire to the place? I'd better tell . . .

No, I'm not going to tell Father, or David, and let them take risks. I'm not going myself, either. If he does set fire to the place, the rain will put it out long before it could reach here. As long as nobody can get in here . . .

She wanted to make sure the doors were all locked, the safety catches on the windows. She went out of her room, moving swiftly, her feet in slippers, and along the hall to the stairs. And in the hall below, she saw Bee, cautiously sliding the chain off the door. She ran down to her.

"Bee," she said, very low. "Where are you going?"

"Out," Bee answered.

She was wearing a transparent, light blue raincoat, her pale blonde hair, parted on the side, hung loose to her shoulders, her blue eyes were narrowed, her mouth had a scornful twist. She looked beautiful and terrible, to Lucia.

"It's raining, Bee. I don't want you to go out."

"I'm sorry, but I'm going," said Bee.

It was plain enough now.

"No," Lucia said. "You can't."

Bee began to turn the doorknob, but Lucia caught her wrist.

"Bee, you want to meet that man."

"All right, I am going to meet Ted," Bee said. "You won't let me go in to New York any more, but I called him up and told him to come here. At least I'm going to explain to him."

"What's this! What's this!" cried old Mr. Harper from the doorway of the sitting room.

Nobody answered him. He stood there, lean and soldierly, with his neat white mustache and his clear blue eyes, an open book in one hand.

"What's this?" he asked again.

"Mother refuses to let me go out of this house," said Bee.

"Your mother's right, Beatrice. Too late, and it's pouring rain."

"Grandpa," Bee said. "I've got a special reason for going out and Mother knows it."

Lucia could see now what the child's tactics were to be. She was counting upon her grandfather's immense indulgence for her, hoping to use it against her mother.

"You take your mother's advice, Beatrice," he said. "Best thing."

"It's *not!* She doesn't understand anything about this. She hasn't any faith in me. She thinks I'm a sort of juvenile delinquent."

"Come, now!" said Mr. Harper.

"She does! Ted's come all the way out here to see me."

"A man?" asked Mr. Harper. "Where is he?"

"In the boathouse. I want to see him for a few moments."

"Your mother's perfectly right, Beatrice. If you want to see this fellow, have him come to the house."

"He couldn't. Not after the way Mother's treated him."

"Beatrice, if your mother doesn't approve of this fellow, she has some good reason, you can be sure of that."

"No!" cried Bee. "I asked him to come, and I'm going to see him, just for a few moments."

"Afraid not, m'dear."

Oh, Bee, darling! Don't look like that! Lucia cried in her heart. As if we were enemies . . . Under the light in the ceiling the child's pale hair glistened, the blue raincoat glittered, she looked so beautiful, so delicate, and so desperate.

"Do you mean," Bee said slowly, "that you and Mother would stop me by force from doing what I think is right?"

"It's not going to come to that, m'dear," he said. "You're going to be a sensible girl and not worry your mother. You know she's thinking only of——"

"Oh, *stop* it!" Bee cried, stamping her foot. "I *won't* . . . I won't . . ."

She began to cry, she tossed her head as if the tears stung her; she turned around and went running up the stairs. Her door slammed.

I hope she won't wake up David, Lucia thought. I shouldn't like him to know anything at all about this.

"Now . . ." her father said. He laid his hand on her shoulder, and a great sense of comfort came to her. "Have you a nice book to read, Lucia?"

"I'm writing to Tom, Father."

"Run along and finish your letter, m'dear," he said. "I'll be down here to see that everything's all right."

She understood what his words implied. He would stay in the sitting room, in a spot where he could watch the stairs, all night if he thought it was necessary. She trusted him as she trusted her own heart. She trusted even his thoughts. He would not misjudge that poor, reckless, furious child.

She kissed him on the cheek. "Good night, Father," she said, and went up the stairs to her own room.

DEAR TOM:

David is sending you some snaps he took of this house, so that you'll have a better idea. It's really very nice. The victory garden isn't doing so very well, though. The soil is too sandy. But the tomatoes are coming along . . .

Her writing was neat and small. It took so very many words to fill a V-mail page. I'm so *slow*, she thought. I'm stupid. I've done so badly with Bee.

The wind had died down and the rain fell straight now, pattering on the roof. A door closed. That's the front door! she thought. Ted's got in!

She hurried out into the hall and from the head of the stairs she saw her father taking off his overcoat. She ran down.

"I went to the boathouse, m'dear," he said. "I had a few words with this fellow. Very unsavory character, I'd call him. Inclined to be troublesome. When I told him to leave the premises, he refused. But I dealt with him. To tell you the truth, I pushed him off into the water."

He was pleased with himself.

"Water's no more than four feet deep there," he said. "Wouldn't drown a child. Won't do the fellow any harm. Do him good. Cool him off."

He patted her shoulder.

"Yes . . ." he said. "I sent him off with a flea in his ear."

Chapter Two

To wake up extra early in the morning was always a delight to Lucia Holley. It gave her an exquisite sense of freedom and privacy. She could do whatever she pleased, while all the others were sleeping.

This morning she waked at five o'clock. For a moment she lay thinking with a heavy heart about Bee; but life and energy were strong in her, and she could not lie still. She got up and put on a black wool bathing suit and a white rubber helmet. She took her rope sandals in her hand and went down the stairs barefoot. David made such a fuss about her swimming alone.

"Anyone that's water-wise," he said, severely, "wouldn't do that."

"I *am* water-wise," Lucia said. "I've been swimming since I was a baby."

"Nobody ought to go swimming all alone," he said. "And anyway, the water's too cold the beginning of May. I wish you wouldn't *do* it."

She felt sorry to do anything that might worry David. But he never wakes up before half-past seven or eight, she thought, and by that time I'll be all dried and dressed. He'll never know, and this is such a wonderful time of day.

She unchained the front door and went out, and sitting on the steps, she put on her sandals. It was a gray morning, but fresh and somehow promising, not like the beginning of a rainy day. I'll row out a little way, she thought. And she thought that when she would be swimming in the gray water, under the soft sky, she would think of some new and better way to talk to Bee.

Something else to offer her, she thought. If I don't let the poor child go in to her art school, what *is* she going to do? I'll have to branch out. I'll have to meet some of the people here, on Bee's account. But I'm so poor at that. It's so hard without Tom.

She had married at eighteen, and she had never gone anywhere without Tom, never had thought of such a thing. And before her marriage, she lived with her mother and father, a tranquil, happy home life with very little going out. She was by nature friendly and uncritical, but she had very little to say for herself. She had no talent for social life and no desire for it.

And that's wrong, she thought. With a daughter Bee's age, it's my *duty* to do things. Maybe I could get Father to go around with me and call on people . . . Maybe Father and I could join the Yacht Club here.

The boathouse was a queer-looking structure, a long wooden tunnel over a cement basin where the boats were moored, and attached to it, on the landward end, a little two-storied cottage with a porch. Ideal for a chauffeur or a couple, the real-estate agent had said, only Lucia had no chauffeur or couple, only Sibyl, who did not care to live out here.

The wooden wall of the tunnel led to an opening with a ramp. She went down this, into the dimness where the rowboat, the canoe, and the motorboat were moored to iron staples. They had all swung out to the end of their ropes, following the ebb tide, and she began to pull in the rowboat. It came as if reluctant, and as she stepped into it, she saw the body.

It was a man, face down in the motorboat, in a strange and dreadful position, his legs sprawled across the thwart, his head and shoulders raised by something. She could not see his face, but something about him, the shape of his head perhaps, made her almost sure it was Ted Darby. And she was almost sure he was dead.

Almost sure was not good enough. She stepped into the motorboat, and it was Ted Darby, and he was dead. He had fallen on a spare anchor, half upended on the seat, and it had pierced his throat.

Father did that, she thought.

She stood in the gently rocking boat, feet apart for balance, tall and long-legged in her white robe. Of course it means the police, she thought. Then Father will have to know that he did this. They'll find out why Ted came here, and Bee will be dragged into it. And I shan't be able to keep it from Tom. Not possibly. It'll be in the tabloids.

It will be so horrible, she thought. For poor little Bee. For Tom. For David. But worst of all for Father. He'll have to go to court. He'll be blamed. He'll be so shocked, so humiliated.

If I were able to get rid of Ted, she thought, I would do it. If I could think of any way to save us all . . .

I could do it, she thought, if I could get him off the anchor.

Standing there, swaying a little as the boat rocked, she knew that she could get him off. She had the resourcefulness of the mother, the domestic woman, accustomed to emergencies. Again and again she had had to deal with accidents, sudden illnesses, breakdowns. For years she had been the person who was responsible in an emergency. She had enough physical strength for this job. What she lacked was the spirit for it. I *couldn't* touch him, she thought.

That's nonsense, she told herself. I thought I couldn't possibly kill old Tiger with gas. But I did. When that laundress had a fit and we were all alone, in the house, I did something about it. When David fell down the cellar stairs and just lay there with blood all over his eyes . . . No, I can do this.

It was very difficult, for the body had begun to stiffen. It was very dreadful. When she got Ted down in the bottom of the boat, her breathing was like sobbing. She got a tarpaulin out of a locker, and spread it over him; then she cast off and started the engine.

The noise was stupendous, terrifying in this enclosed space, in the early-morning quiet. She had trouble, too. The engine started and stopped and started again. Bang, *bang*, puttputtputt. *Bang*. They'll hear it at the house and somebody will come, she thought. Even when she was under way, the noise was atrociously loud.

She steered through the narrow inlet through the reeds and out into the open water of the Sound, in a world gray, soft, and quiet. There was no other craft in sight. She had already made up her mind to take Ted to Simm's Island. She had decided upon the best spot. On the side of the small island that faced the mainland there was a row of bleached little summer bungalows, all empty, as far as she knew. But I shan't go near them, she thought.

She and David and Bee had come here for a picnic lunch a week ago. They had been looking then for a nice place.

She was looking now for a half-remembered place, so far from nice that no one would be likely to go there. It would be dreadful if a child were to find him, she thought.

Here was the place, a narrow strip of sand, and behind it a stretch of marsh where the tall reeds stirred in the breeze. She stopped the engine, and dropped the anchor. She drew a long breath and set to work.

Ted was very slight, but even at that, it was hard enough to lift him out of the boat. Then she took him under the shoulders and dragged him to the marsh, well in among the tall reeds. He looked grotesque and horrible with his arms and legs sprawled out; she tried to straighten him and could not, and she began to cry. There he lay, staring at the sky.

I can't leave him like this, she thought. There was a big blue bandanna in the pocket of her terry robe. She took it out and dried her eyes with it, and spread it over his face. But the breeze lifted it at once. There were no stones here to anchor it down. She knelt beside him frowning, still crying. Then with her strong sharp teeth she tore two corners of the bandanna into strips, and tied it, cater-cornered over his face, to two reeds.

It's better than nothing, she thought, and went back to the boat. The engine started easily this time. When she was out in the open water she stopped it again and cleaned the bottom of the boat with an oily rag. There was very little blood. I hope it was quick, she thought. I hope he wasn't there a long time—alone . . .

She tied the robe tight around her waist and turned in the lapels across her chest, for the breeze seemed chilly now. She started the engine, headed for home. It's done, she told herself. I'm going to put it out of my mind. But suddenly she thought of the bandanna. Well, nobody could identify it, she thought. It's just one I bought in the ten-cent store ages ago. There must be thousands and thousands exactly like it. Fingerprints? I don't think they get fingerprints from cloth of any kind. Anyhow I could say I'd left the bandanna on the island the day we had the picnic.

Anyhow, I can't help it now. It's done. And I'm not going to brood about it. I'm not going to think about it at all.

As she approached the boathouse, she felt a faint shock of dismay to see David standing there, thin and slouching, in blue trunks and a khaki windbreaker. But she recovered herself at once. It's just as well to have to start right in, she thought.

"Hello, David," she said, cheerfully.

"Hello," he said unsmiling.

As the boat glided into the tunnel, he moved along to the ramp, and was waiting to help her out.

"I couldn't believe my ears," he said, "when I heard the engine start. I thought someone was stealing the boat and I got down here as quick as I could, and I saw you scooting away."

"I like the early morning," she said.

"That's all right," said David. "But why didn't you take the rowboat, like you always do?"

"Well, I thought I'd like the motorboat for a change."

"Well, I ask you not to do it again," said David. "It's dangerous. You don't know one darn thing about that engine. If it stalled or even the least little thing went wrong, you'd be absolutely helpless."

"I didn't go far," said Lucia.

"Well, I ask you not to do it," said David. "It's darned eccentric, anyhow."

"There's nothing so terrible about being eccentric once in a while," said Lucia.

"Personally," said David, "I shouldn't like any of the fellows I know out here to see you scooting around in a motorboat at half-past five in the morning."

David's like Father, Lucia thought. But he looks like Tom with those furry ginger eyelashes and those nice green eyes. He's only fifteen. Only a child. But in three more years . . . if the war goes on for three more years . . .

Again and again and again that thought would come to her, piercing her heart. She put her arms around his thin shoulders.

"I'm quite sure none of your friends saw me, dear," she said. "But I won't do it again, if it worries you."

"Well, that's good," he said.

"Let's go along to the house and get some breakfast."

"Sibyl won't be down yet."

"I can manage," said Lucia.

She took her arm away from his shoulders and they walked in side by side.

"What's the matter with Bee?" he asked.

"What do you mean, David?"

"You certainly must have noticed it," he said. "Of course most of it's an act. She's always putting on an act. But something's been bothering her lately, all right."

"Doesn't she ever talk to you about things, David? You used to talk everything over together."

"I don't encourage that," said David.

"It does people good to talk over their troubles to—"

"Well, it doesn't do me good to listen to them," he said with unexpected vehemence. "I don't like anything that's sappy and emotional and all, and I don't want to get mixed up in things like that. Not now, or any other time."

He held open the screen door and she went past him into Sibyl's beautiful kitchen. The sun was breaking through the clouds; a shaft lay upon the green and white linoleum floor. It was a lovely thing to be getting breakfast for David.

Chapter Three

"We could wait till tomorrow," said Sibyl. "Only this is the day for the chicken man."

"Then I'll get you a taxi," said Lucia.

"Better if you go, ma'am," said Sibyl, standing by the kitchen table, tall, portly, her dark face impassive.

"You're a much better marketer than I am," said Lucia.

"My business to be so," said Sibyl, quietly. "But the chicken man don't like colored people. Don't hesitate to say so."

"Has he ever said anything to you, Sibyl?"

"Yes, ma'am," said Sibyl.

"We won't deal with him any more," said Lucia.

"He's the only one got any chickens," said Sibyl.

"Then we'll do without chickens for the rest of the summer."

Sibyl smiled a smile, gentle, infinitely affectionate.

"No, ma'am," she said. "If you go, maybe you can get us two nice roasting chickens and I'll cook them Saturday and we'll have a chicken salad Sunday. I'll give you the list, ma'am."

They had been together, day in and day out, for eight years, in complete harmony. Sibyl knew that Lucia was not the wise, thrifty housewife the family believed her to be. Sibyl remembered the things Lucia forgot, found the things that Lucia lost, covered up Lucia's absent-mindedness, advised her, warned her. She had lent Lucia money, to conceal a shockingly careless overdraft, and had herself gone to the police about the chauffeur Lucia could not bring herself to accuse.

She knew Lucia better than any one else did. But Lucia knew curiously little about Sibyl. She did not know Sibyl's age, or where she had been born, what family she had, or what friends. She had no idea where Sibyl went on her afternoons off, or what she did. Simply, she loved and trusted Sibyl without reservation.

"Well, maybe I can speak to the chicken man," she said.

"No, ma'am," said Sibyl. "Can't change this world."

From where she stood, Lucia could see her father at his breakfast in the dining room, the soft collar of his blue shirt revealing his lean old neck. He was wearing the black and white checked jacket he had bought in London years ago, and cherished so fondly, getting it relined and patched up again and again. Rather have a really decent jacket like this even if it was a bit shabby than a cheap flimsy new one, he often said.

He could very well have got himself a new one, not cheap and flimsy, but his daughter never pointed this out to him. He thinks it's more English to be shabby, she thought, and why shouldn't he if he wants?

I'm so glad I was able to get Ted away, she thought. Now no matter what happens, I don't see how Father could even find out what he did last night, or be connected with it in any way. Nobody will ever know.

She went in and kissed the top of his neat white head.

"Father," she said, "I think it would be better not to let Bee know that you saw that man last night."

"I didn't see him," said Mr. Harper.

"But, Father . . . !"

"Too dark," said he, pleased with the joke. "Don't worry, my dear. I shan't tell Beatrice. And I don't think we'll be troubled again by the young gentleman."

Bee was coming down the stairs. She came straight into the kitchen.

"Good morning, Mother," she said. "Good morning, Sibyl. Is my orange juice in the icebox?"

"Yes, Miss Bee."

Bee brought out the bowl that held the full pint of orange and lemon juice combined which was an essential part of her new Vitabelle diet and carried it into the dining room.

"Good morning, Grandpa," she said.

This, obviously, was to be her attitude, polite, cool, aloof; no smiles for her oppressors.

"Going in to your school today?" Harper asked, surprised by her appearance in blue overalls and white shirt.

"I'm not allowed to go any more," Bee answered, very clearly.

"Oh . . . I see!" he said. "Number of pretty scenes around here that you could paint, I should think."

She gave the smile Lucia, watching from the kitchen, hated to see. The child was so lovely, with her soft fair hair, her delicate skin, her fine little features, but she rouged her mouth into a sort of square, and when she smiled this way, with her lips scarcely parted, and her eyes narrowed, she looked almost ugly.

She couldn't really have cared so very much for a man like Ted, Lucia thought. Of course she'll be terribly upset when she hears that he's dead, but she'll get over it. She's so *very* young. Poor Bee . . . I must do something about branching out, finding more friends for her. And there's no reason now why she shouldn't go back to the art school, only that I can't tell her. Can I just say I changed my mind? Or had I better wait until Ted gets into the papers?

She telephoned for a taxi and changed into a costume suitable for the village, a blue and white checked gingham dress, a blue belt, blue sandals, a wide black straw hat. Sibyl had the list ready for her and when the cab came, off she went, with the big green denim market bag.

I'll tell Bee this afternoon that I've changed my mind, she thought. Then she can go in to her school tomorrow. It may be quite a while before Ted gets into the papers, and there's no reason why she should stay home, poor child. Is she going to mind very much, when she finds out? It's so hard to understand how she could possibly have cared, even the least little bit, for a man like that. So cheap and sneering . . .

It was a morning of frustration. The chicken man would sell her only one chicken, and a smallish one at that. There was no margarine, no sugar. She could not get the brand of soap flakes Sibyl particularly wanted. The only potatoes she found were old and soft and sprouting. The only cigarettes were an unheard-of variety.

She could not get the tooth paste her father wanted. She could not get the magazines David had asked for. Bee's shoes, promised for last week by the shoemaker, still stood untouched, on a shelf. She went from one shop to another, the bag growing heavier and heavier. She was hot, flushed and tired, but still with her air of earnest politeness. She stood patiently in line at counters, she engaged in conversation with other housewives, she was zealous with her ration stamps.

When she had got what she could, she had a big paper bag in addition to the market bag. They'd hate me too much in the bus with all this, she thought, and crossed the main street of the village, pulled down by the bag, to the railway station, where three taxis stood.

"Got to wait for the train, lady," the first driver said.

He could put three or even four passengers in together; he was not interested in this single fare.

"If I drive you out to Plattsville," said the second, "I got to come all the way back empty. It don't pay me."

"Well, suppose I pay a little extra . . . ?" Lucia said, hot and tired.

"Well . . ." said the driver, "we're not supposed to do that. I'd have to charge you two dollars and a half."

That was outrageous. For a moment she contemplated trying the third, but he would realize that he was the last resort and he might take advantage of it. He might be worse.

"All right," she said, and got into the cab.

Just at that moment the train came in and her driver waited. A little crowd of people descended; the two other cabs pulled up to drive away, and a man came, leisurely and deliberately, toward Lucia's taxi. He was a stout man, in a gray suit with the jacket open. He walked with a sort of roll, bearing his portly stomach proudly.

"Know where some people named Holley live, son?" he asked the driver.

"Nope," said the driver. "You might ask the ticket office."

"You run along and do the asking, son," said the stout man.

Lucia sat back in a corner, looking at him in unreasoning dismay. His eyes . . . she said to herself. They were very pale eyes, light-lashed, with a curious blankness, as if he were blind. He's a detective, she thought, and he's come about Ted.

"I got a fare," said the driver, "the other cabs'll be coming back."

"You go find out where the Holleys live, son," said the stout man, in the same even, indifferent voice, and it increased Lucia's dismay to see that the far from obliging young driver was prepared to do as he was told. Everyone would do what that man said.

"I'm going out there," she said.

The stout man gave her a glance, a thorough one from head to foot.

"You told me the Maxwell place," cried the driver, shocked and aggrieved.

"I know," Lucia said. "But we've rented it."

The stout man opened the door of the cab and got in. He sat down beside Lucia with his knees apart, taking up a good deal of room.

"Get going, son," he said.

He's one of those horrible detectives that you see in the movies, Lucia thought. He's . . . the word sprang up in her mind. He's merciless, she thought. He'd be merciless to Father.

"Your name Holley?" he asked.

"Yes."

"You got a sister or daughter name of Beatrice?"

"Yes," she answered again.

"She's the one I want to see," he said.

"Well . . . what about?"

"I'll take it up with her," he said.

"I'd rather you didn't," said Lucia. "I'm her mother. I can tell you anything she could tell you."

"She's the one I came out to see," he said. "Beatrice Holley."

"You might as well tell me what you want to see her about. She'll tell me herself, later on."

"Think so?"

"Yes, I know it. I wish you wouldn't talk to her. If you'd please talk to me instead . . . ?"

"It's Beatrice Holley I want," he said.

Something like panic assailed Lucia. He'll tell Bee that Ted's been found, she thought. It must be that. What else could bring him here? He'll ask her questions and questions, and she'll tell him things that'll get in the papers. I can't let her see this man, alone.

"My daughter's a minor," she said. "I'm sorry but I can't let you see her."

He turned his head and gave her another glance, his light lashes flickering up and down. Then he turned away again.

"That won't work," he said.

It was intolerable that Bee should have to endure this.

"I'm going to send for my lawyer," said Lucia.

He did not trouble to answer that; he sat with his double chin resting on his chest, looking straight before him, thinking his own thoughts. Lucia was of absolutely no interest to him.

They were in sight of the house now. David was strolling across the lawn of coarse grass; when he saw the cab he stopped and waited.

"What's the fare?" said the stout man.

"Dollar," said the driver, and the stout man gave him a dollar, no tip. He opened the door of the cab and got out without a glance at Lucia. He was speaking to David before she got her dollar out of her purse.

"Two-fifty was the rate," said the driver.

She gave him another fifty cents and got out, with her two big bags. The stout man was standing in front of the house.

"If you talk to my daughter, I'm going to be there, too," she said.

He didn't answer her. She stood there with the bags, utterly at a loss, but determined to protect Bee as best she could. The screen door opened and Bee came out. She looked with a frown of surprise at the two standing on the lawn, and ran down the steps.

"You wanted to see me?" she asked.

"You Beatrice Holley?"

"Bee—" Lucia began. "Don't."

"It's just something about the school, Mother," said Bee.

"It isn't!" said Lucia.

"It isn't," said the man. "I told the boy that. Makes it easier. No. I came to ask about my good friend Ted Darby."

"Well . . . Who are you?" Bee asked.

"The name's Nagle."

"Well . . . What do you want to ask?"

"Bee . . . !" said Lucia. "Don't!"

He's not a detective, she thought. He's—I don't know—a crook, a gangster, something horrible.

"Ted came out to see you last night," said Nagle.

"What if he did?" said Bee.

"He never came home again," said Nagle.

The statement was shocking to Lucia and frightening. But Bee was not alarmed.

"You mean he didn't go back to his hotel?" she said. "Then he probably went to visit someone. He has plenty of friends."

"Did he tell you he was going to visit somebody?"

"My daughter didn't see him last night," said Lucia.

"You saw him?"

"No. Nobody saw him."

"You're saying he didn't come here?"

"I don't know whether he came or not. I'm just saying that none of us saw him."

He turned to Bee.

"You called him up," he said. "You asked him to come out here last night. Well?"

"Well?" Bee replied. "I can't see what right you have to come here and ask me questions."

She was not in the least afraid of Nagle. She met his pale eyes steadily.

"Why didn't you see him?" asked Nagle.

"That's my own business," she said. "Come in, Mother, let's——"

"Wait!" said Nagle. "It's not that easy. I want everything you've got about my good friend Ted Darby. Names of any friends he's told you——"

"I'm not going to tell you anything at all," said Bee. "You can wait till he gets back and ask him."

"If you know where he is," said Nagle, "you'd better tell me."

"I'll take the bags in, ma'am," said Sibyl's voice behind Lucia.

She took the bags and walked away, erect and stately.

"I shan't tell you anything at all," said Bee.

"That's just too bad," said Nagle. "That's too bad for Ted."

"What do you mean?" Bee demanded. "Are you threatening him?"

"I ask questions," said Nagle. "I don't answer."

"That goes for me too," said Bee.

She's—tough, Lucia thought astonished. That slender girl in slacks, her light hair down to her shoulders, that child, who had lived all her life at home, protected and cherished, was talking now like a tough girl in a movie, looking like one, too, with her eyes narrowed and her fine mouth scornful.

"Okay! Okay!" said Nagle, and turned away.

Lucia stood looking after him, with dread and dismay in her heart. He'll come back, she thought. This is only the beginning. . . .

Chapter Four

"Dear Tom," Lucia wrote, "it was so very nice to get an air-mail from you this afternoon, especially a letter telling about the details of your life and your friends and your men. Things like that seem to bring you so much closer, Tom."

Only they didn't, really. I haven't much imagination, she thought, regretfully. I can't imagine Tom being a naval officer. I think of him as he was before he left, over two years ago, and probably he's not like that any more. No, he'll have changed, and I'll be just the same.

She went on with her dull, earnest, loving letter. Thank goodness Tom doesn't expect me to be wonderful, she thought. He knows what I'm like. When Tom had first met her she had been seventeen and still in school, a very earnest student but never excelling in anything, never a leader in anything. She liked everyone and was interested in no one. You're the hardest girl in the world to make love to, Tom had told her once. You're just so blamed friendly.

When she was eighteen they were married. When she was nineteen Bee had been born, and that was that. She had always been faintly disappointed in herself, disappointed in school because she had not been remarkable, disappointed when she married because she had not become the perfect housekeeper, most of all disappointed in herself as a mother. Whenever she visited her children's school she felt singularly inept among the other mothers. Simply not *real,* she thought.

I don't cope with things. That Nagle . . . Bee wasn't at all afraid of him. But I was. I am now. Suppose he tells the police that Ted was coming here . . . ? Well, I'll say he didn't come. But if they start asking Father questions . . . I'm pretty sure he's never heard Ted's name. But he'd say, yes, there was a man, and I sent him away with a flea in his ear.

If Father knew he'd killed Ted, he'd tell the police at once. He's like that. I know just how he'd talk. My dear, I am always prepared to accept the consequences of my acts. The full consequences. And then, of course, Bee would be dragged into it. And Tom would have to know. Why can't I look after my own daughter?

Lying in bed in the dark, a desperate, almost panic compulsion *to do something* rose in her. But she mastered it at once. Don't be frantic, she told herself. Just one day at a time. Just take things as they come.

She got up and lit a cigarette; when it was finished, she stubbed it out carefully and closed her eyes. I'm going to wake up at five o'clock, she told herself.

So she did, but to a morning of wild wind and rain. I'd love a little swim in this weather, she thought, but I'd worry David too much. No . . . I'll take a little walk out of sight of the house.

The idea was strong in her mind that she must stand guard over the house, that she must protect the inmates. She dressed in an old blue flannel skirt, a black sweater and tennis shoes. She tied a white scarf over her hair and went stealthily down the stairs and out of the house.

And out in the rain and the rough wind, she forgot her fears and distress. She went down the drive to the highway and walked up and down, as if patrolling, her skirt flattened against her long legs, her dark face wet and glowing.

"You look like a gypsy," her father said, benevolently, when she came back to the house.

The morning routine went on. The newspaper came and there was nothing about Ted. Old Mr. Harper went out for his constitutional. David went off in the motorboat to visit some friends he had made; Bee was shut in her own room. And Lucia did the things appointed to be done on Thursday. She stripped all the beds, she made out the laundry list. She tidied and dusted the sitting room and the bathroom she shared with Bee. In a blue cotton pinafore, she had an air of serious efficiency; nobody would know that all this was arranged entirely by Sibyl.

Before lunch, she knocked on Bee's door.

"Come in!" said Bee.

She was sitting at a table by the window, drawing, in a candy-striped play suit, her silky hair pushed back from her forehead.

"Bee," said Lucia. "I've been thinking things over . . . I can't bear for you to stay away from your art school, Bee. Go back tomorrow, dear, and I'll simply trust to your . . ."

"If you think you'll stop me from seeing Ted by saying you 'trust' me," said Bee, "you're mistaken."

"Bee, you don't need to be so hostile. Not to me."

"Mother," said Bee, and was silent for a time. "I know you're terribly fond of me. I know you think you're doing what's best for me. But I don't agree with you about *anything*."

"Bee, you do!"

"No. I'm not a fool about Ted. I realize he isn't our kind of person. Daddy wouldn't like him any more than you do. But I want to know all kinds of people. I want to live out in the world. I'd just as soon be *dead*, as have a life like you."

"Bee!" said Lucia, startled, even shocked. "I've got all the things that are most worth having in the world."

"I think your life is *awful,*" said Bee. "I'd rather——"

"Lunch!" called David from the hall, and Bee rose promptly.

"I'm sorry, Mother," Bee went on with a sort of stern regret. "But I'm not like you. I'm not going to have a life like yours. If you can call it a life. Getting married at eighteen, right from school. Never really seeing anything or doing anything. No adventure, no color. I suppose you like feeling safe. Well, *I* don't want to be safe."

"Come on, Mother!" called David.

He was always a little irritated by the private conversations that Lucia had with his sister. He himself never sought private conversations. He was willing to talk to anyone about anything. When the clergyman had come to call, he had shown a disposition to discuss religion with him which Lucia had had trouble in suppressing.

At the lunch table, he discussed the Pacific campaign with his grandfather while Bee sat silent, with a look of faintly amused boredom. I think he's very intelligent, Lucia said to herself. I like the way men talk.

As they were about to leave the table, Sibyl appeared in the doorway.

"The refrigerator is gone again, ma'am," she said, evenly.

"I don't know what you people *do* to that icebox," said Mr. Harper, frowning.

It was an unbreakable convention that whenever the refrigerator went out of order, nobody but Mr. Harper could turn off the gas properly. He now did this, and it was all he could do. He was not at all handy about the house. Neither was David, who was further disqualified by being candidly indifferent.

"Why worry?" he said. "People didn't use to have mechanical iceboxes, and they got on all right."

"Then they had cakes of ice," said Lucia.

"No," said David, reasonably. "Grandpa's told me, plenty of times, that when he was a boy in England, they *never* had any ice. If they specially needed it, if anyone was sick or anything, they had to send to the fishmonger's."

"Well, that's a different climate," said Lucia.

"The temperature's only sixty-six now," said David. "You couldn't call that so very hot."

He strolled away. Mr. Harper had already gone.

"I'll telephone the company," said Lucia.

"Yes, ma'am," said Sibyl, with the same doubt and heaviness.

This recurring trouble with the icebox was a catastrophe they both dreaded. Lucia went to the telephone and she got that girl.

"Holley?" said the girl. "All right. I'll put it down."

"When do you think the man will come?"

"I haven't any idea," said the girl. "He takes all the calls in order. You'll just have to wait for your turn."

"Naturally," said Lucia, coldly. "I simply wanted to know if you could give me any idea . . ."

"He'll come when it's your turn," said the girl. "This company doesn't play any favorites."

"Damn you," said Lucia, but not aloud, and returned to the kitchen. "They won't say when he's coming," she told Sibyl. "I suppose we'd better have the fish tonight . . . ?"

"Better had," said Sibyl. "They won't like fish two nights running, but if the man doesn't come this afternoon . . ."

They both knew he would not come this afternoon.

"Well, as long as he comes before the week end . . ." said Lucia, and was silent for a moment, thinking about it. "I think I'll take a little nap," she said, apologetically. "But call me if anything turns up."

"Yes, ma'am," said Sibyl, with indulgence. She approved of Lucia's taking naps.

But Lucia was longer than usual in falling asleep today. If the Nagle man comes back, she thought, I don't want Bee to see him alone. I don't want Father to see him at all. Ever. Maybe I ought to stay awake, in case something happens . . .

In the end, drowsiness overwhelmed her. She lay stretched out, long and lean in a shrunken gray flannel dressing gown, her hands clasped over her head.

"Mrs. Holley, ma'am . . . !" Sibyl's voice said, insistently.

"Yes?" said Lucia, sitting up.

Sibyl stood beside her, grave and impassive.

"There's a man here wants to see you," she said.

"What man, Sibyl?"

"Wouldn't give his name," said Sibyl. "Just said he wanted to see you about something personal."

Their eyes met in a long look.

"Sibyl . . . What's he like?"

They were still looking straight at each other, and into Sibyl's amber-flecked dark eyes came a troubled shadow. She was a reticent woman. It was hard for her to find words for her thoughts.

"He don't look like a man you'd know," she said.

It's Nagle, Lucia thought. I knew he'd come back.

"He's on the veranda," Sibyl went on. "I can send him away."

"I'd better see him," said Lucia and got up, standing tall and straight on her narrow bare feet.

"You don't have to, ma'am," said Sibyl. "Told him I didn't know if you were in."

"No. I'd better see him," Lucia repeated. "Tell him I'll be down in a moment, please."

"Let him in?" Sibyl asked, and again their eyes met.

"Yes. Yes, please," said Lucia.

She had to let him into her house, for she dared not keep him out. She stood motionless until she heard the front door close, and then she began to dress quickly and carelessly, in the checked gingham dress that was limp now. He's in, she said to herself. He's in the house.

She went down the stairs and into the sitting room. But the man who stood there was not Nagle.

"Mrs. Holley?" he asked.

He was a big man, broad shouldered and narrow flanked, very well dressed, in a dark suit, a sober and expensive necktie. He was a handsome man, or could be, or had been. But there was something curiously blurred about him, like a fine drawing partly erased. His strong-boned face looked tired. His dark blue eyes looked somehow dim.

"My name is Donnelly," he said and his voice was muffled.

"Yes?" said Lucia evenly.

Maybe it's nothing, she told herself. Maybe it's just about the insurance. Or selling War Bonds. Or, something just ordinary.

But she could not believe it. He came from some other world, the world of Ted Darby and Nagle, strange and unknown to her as the banks of Lethe.

"I'd like a few words with you," he said, and jerked his dark head toward the open door behind her.

"Well . . . what about?" she asked, with an attempt at defiance.

He moved light on his feet, he reached past her and closed the door.

"You'll be wanting these letters," he said.

"What letters?"

They were standing close to each other, facing each other; she looked up at him, still attempting that defiance, and he looked at her absently.

"The letters your daughter wrote to Ted Darby," he said. "The price is five thousand dollars. Cash."

Chapter Five

She was aware that she was not really thinking at all. Not yet.

"Well . . . Sit down, please," she said.

He waited until she was seated, and then he drew up a chair, facing her, and sat down, carefully hitching up his trousers. He was remarkably neat, his dark hair neat on his narrow skull, his big hands well kept, his shoes gleaming. He was so strangely, so dreadfully indifferent, simply waiting. A blackmailer, she thought. This is blackmail.

"My daughter . . ." she said. "There's nothing in her letters . . ."

"Would you like to see one?" he asked.

He took a handsome pigskin wallet out of an inside pocket, drew out a sheaf of folded papers, and looked through them. He selected one and handed it to her.

TED:

I just wasn't alive until I met you. But you came like a fresh wind blowing through a stuffy room. I don't know, Ted, if I can make up my mind to do what you asked yesterday. But just the fact that you *did* ask, and that you thought I had the courage to take such a chance makes me feel proud.

Ted, I'm thinking about it. I'm not sentimental; you know that. But just the same it is hard to break entirely with the past, and go against everyone and everything you were taught.

See you Friday, Ted, and maybe by that time I'll have made up my mind.

BEATRICE

The clear beautiful printing Bee used made the words so stark . . .

"That doesn't mean anything," said Lucia. "She's only a child. That doesn't mean—anything."

"It looks like something," he said, and held out his hand for the letter.

"No!" she said, putting it behind her. "I shan't give it to you. I—the police will make you give me those letters."

He didn't bother to answer that. He sat leaning forward a little, holding the handsome wallet open on his knee. Simply waiting.

"I'm going to put this in my lawyer's hands," Lucia said. And she had a vision of Albert Hendry, Tom's lawyer, ineffably distinguished, listening to the story of Bee's disastrous folly.

"Why do you not pay the money and forget all about it?" asked Donnelly. "There's nothing else you can do at all."

"No!" said Lucia. "I wouldn't pay blackmail. Never!"

"There's someone else will," he said.

"Who?"

"Your father, maybe."

"No!" she cried. "No! You can't . . . No!"

She checked herself. She tried to breathe evenly. She tried to think.

"How did *you* get hold of these letters?" she asked.

"Darby wanted to borrow a bit," said Donnelly, "and he left me the letters till he'd pay me back."

"Do you mean that *he*——?"

"Oh, he had it in mind to make the girl pay for them," said Donnelly.

His tone was not at all threatening. There was no hint of violence in him. But his matter-of-fact acceptance of this incredible treachery, this criminal demand, seemed to her infinitely more alarming than violence and infinitely more difficult to meet. The word "blackmail" disturbed him not at all.

"Darby's run out on me now," he said, as if explaining a business affair. "He went off without a word. And I cannot afford to lose what I lent him."

He doesn't know what happened to Ted, she thought. When he finds out, will that change things? Make this better? Or worse? If I could only, *only* think this out.

The rain rattled against the window, the room seemed close, filled with a gray light. Here she sat with this man, this criminal, so well dressed, so unclamorous . . .

"I'll have to have time to think this over," she said coldly.

"I'm going to Montreal," he said, again with that reasonable air of explaining matters to her. "I'll need the money before I go."

"I haven't got five thousand dollars," she said.

"You'll think of a way to lay hands on it," he said.

"No . . . No. When you get that, you'll ask for more."

"I would not," he said, simply.

"No! There's nothing in those letters. Nothing at all wrong."

"They would look wrong," he said.

"Don't you realize," she began, when the door opened and old Mr. Harper entered.

"Oh," he said, "sorry, m'dear. I didn't know . . . Getting near teatime, I thought . . ."

Donnelly had risen; he stood there, like any polite stranger, waiting to be introduced.

"Father . . ." she said, "this is Mr. Donnelly."

"How d'you do, sir?" said Mr. Harper.

But he was not satisfied with this. He wanted, naturally, to know who Mr. Donnelly was and why he was here.

"From Tom's office," she said, in her desperation.

"Ha! From Tom's office," said Mr. Harper, and held out his hand. "Glad to see you, sir. Sit down! Sit down!"

No! No! No! Lucia cried to herself.

"Mr. Donnelly's just leaving, Father," she said.

"You can wait for a cup of tea, eh, Donnelly? Or a highball?"

"Thank you, sir," said Donnelly, and sat down again.

"How is everything in the office?" asked Mr. Harper.

"I couldn't tell you," Donnelly answered, "for I left there three years ago. Government work."

"I see!" said Mr. Harper. "Lucia, m'dear, d'you think you could ask Sibyl to bring along the tea? Or if you'd prefer a whisky and soda, Donnelly?"

"Tea, if you please," said Donnelly.

There were no bells in the house to summon Sibyl. Lucia rose and went out to the kitchen. As she pushed open the swing door, she saw Sibyl standing at a table under the window, cutting raw carrots into little flowers, her dark face in profile was proud and melancholy. She turned at the sound of Lucia's step.

"Sibyl . . ." Lucia said, and could get no further. She was crushed and overwhelmed by this catastrophe.

"What's wrong, ma'am?" asked Sibyl with compassion in her eyes.

"He's staying . . ." Lucia answered.

"That man?"

"Yes. Father's asked him to tea."

Sibyl, too, was silent for a moment.

"We must just do the best we can," said Sibyl. "Don't fret, ma'am."

"But he's——"

"Yes, ma'am," said Sibyl. "I know."

She turned and put the carrots into a bowl of cold water.

"You go back now, ma'am. I'll bring in the tea. Don't fret, ma'am. Sometimes there's good luck in this life. No harm to hope for it."

That was language Lucia could understand. Her father and her husband never spoke like that. In the blackest days of the war, old Mr. Harper had never had the slightest doubt of England's victory; he considered doubt to be a form of treason. And Tom, when he went away, had had the same resolute optimism.

"I'll come through all right," he had said, looking at her pale, averted face. "It's half the battle, Lucia," he had said, "to feel hopeful. Sure that you're lucky."

She did not believe that. She believed that a shell or a bullet could strike a brave and hopeful man as readily as a miserable one. She did not believe that the guilty were always punished; or the innocent always spared. She believed, like Sibyl, that life was incalculable, and that the only shield against injustice was courage.

She had courage.

"All right, Sibyl," she said and turned away.

Old Mr. Harper was having a good time. He was talking about the First World War to Donnelly who, it seemed, had been in it. In France and Belgium he had seen some of the English regiments whose names were glorious and almost sacred to the old man. Donnelly was far from eloquent, but his few words entirely satisfied Mr. Harper.

"Have you ever been in England, Donnelly?"

"I was in and out of Liverpool for nearly a year, sir."

"Oh, Liverpool . . ." said Mr. Harper, politely dismissing that city. "Never been there myself. But London . . . Ever been in London, Donnelly?"

"I have, sir. It is a fine city."

"I imagine it very changed now, Donnelly."

"It has a right to be," said Donnelly, gravely.

Lucia sat on the sofa with the tea table drawn up before her. She poured tea; when her father remembered to include her in the conversation, she responded quickly, with a bright smile. If I could only go out and take a walk, she thought, I'd be able to think. I've got to think. I've got to find a way out of this. I've got to stop being so stupid and dazed.

And then, to complete the nightmare, Bee came downstairs.

"Oh . . . !" she said from the doorway, as if surprised to see a stranger here.

But Lucia noticed that she was much more carefully got up than was natural for an ordinary afternoon at home. She was wearing a lemon-colored organdy blouse and a black skirt; she had blue mascara on her lashes and fresh make-up on her mouth.

Go away! Lucia cried in her heart. Don't you come in here . . .

Mr. Harper waited, but his daughter was drinking tea, her eyes lowered.

"This is Mr. Donnelly, Beatrice," he said. "From your father's office. My granddaughter, Donnelly."

Donnelly rose.

"Oh . . . How do you do?" said Bee, and he gave a slight bow.

She sat down on the sofa beside her mother, and lit a cigarette.

"No tea, thank you, Mother. Is there any grape juice?"

"It's too many points," said Lucia.

"Then could I have some iced tea, Mother?"

"I'm sorry, but there's no ice. The refrigerator's out of order."

"What a life!" said Bee laughing.

She wanted to get the attention of this stranger. It would have irritated David, but to Lucia it was heartbreaking. She saw Donnelly glance at her lovely child, an unreadable glance, and then turn to listen to old Mr. Harper, and a fierce, desperate rebellion rose in her.

I let him get in, she thought. There he is, with Bee's letters in his pocket. Trying to blackmail me. I'll get those letters somehow. I'll do something.

Donnelly rose.

"I'll have to be going," he said, "but I'll be in the neighborhood for a while."

"Oh, stopping out here?"

"It is business," said Donnelly. "Mrs. Holley, could I stop by in my car tomorrow around eleven, maybe, and drive you to see the old house we were speaking about?"

His effrontery was beyond belief. Here, under her own roof, in the presence of her father and her daughter, he dared propose this rendezvous. But she had let him get in, and her home was no longer safe.

All right! she thought. All right! She raised her dark eyes and looked straight at him, a hot color in her cheeks, a defiance in her heart.

"Thanks. That would be very nice," she said.

I'll settle with you, all right, she thought. I'll think of something. Just wait and see.

Chapter Six

All right! All right! she thought. Let him take the letters to Father, and see what happens. Just let him try to blackmail Father.

It will be hard for Bee. But Father'll know that there's really nothing to those letters. No matter how they sound. She went to sleep with that in her mind, defiant and resolute.

But when she waked in the early morning, all that was gone. I simply can't trust Father, she thought. He's so upright. He'd probably want to go to the police. We must see this through, my dear. And then the police would connect Bee with Ted, and when they found Ted . . .

No. I'll put Donnelly off. I'll pretend I'm getting the money for him. That'll give me a little more time.

And what was she going to do with this time? Think of something. Do something.

It was a soft, mild morning of pale sunshine. With a regretful thought for David, she put on her bathing suit and went quietly out of the house, and down to the boathouse. She took the rowboat this time; she went out through the tunnel at the narrow inlet through the reeds into the open water. Oh, this is the best thing! she thought and laying the oars in the bottom of the boat, she made a shallow dive into the water.

"Hey!" she cried aloud, because it was so cold. But, in a moment, as she swam, the water no longer felt cold, only exquisitely refreshing. There were gulls flying overhead, and she turned on her back and floated, to watch them, one swooped so low that she could see its fierce face.

She lay floating in the sparkling water, looking with half-closed eyes at the gulls and the little clouds in the soft blue sky. She turned over and swam around the boat twice, happy in the smooth rhythm of her muscles. Just for practice she swam under the boat, in cold shadow for a moment, and came up with the sun again.

A motorboat had started somewhere. David, coming after me? she thought and climbed hastily into the rowboat. But the motorboat was now behind her. It was coming from the island. As she took up the oars she saw it. There was a policeman in uniform behind the wheel and in the stern sat another policeman, and a young man in a gray suit, a big young man with big, outstanding ears and a big bony nose. Motionless, she sat watching them, and the young man turned his head, looking at her; as they passed, she met his eyes, dark, gentle and a little sad.

Then they were gone. The rowboat rocked violently in the swell. They'd found Ted, she thought. *Now* what's going to happen?

She began to row homeward. All right. All right. I'll take things as they come. One at a time. I'm not going to worry. I'm not going to borrow trouble. I'll manage, all right. She took off her rubber cap and let her dark hair blow loose in the wind. She rowed slowly, and let the sun dry her woolen suit.

And if the police come asking questions about Ted, I'll

say he never came near us. Father doesn't know who it was he spoke to. I'd better tell him something this morning.

She got back to her room, unheard by David. She dressed and sat down by the open window. Now, if anybody comes, I'm ready, she thought. I don't care what I say. I don't care how many lies I tell.

She heard Sibyl go creaking down the stairs and a few moments later she followed.

"Certainly hope that laundry man comes today," said Sibyl. "I don't know how Mr. Harper's going to hold out, with only one clean shirt to last him a whole week."

It was like gears meshing. This was the day beginning. This was life.

"I'd better go into New York and try again to get him some more shirts," she said. "And David, too. But they're so scarce and so expensive."

"We could manage," said Sibyl, "if the laundry man'll do what he said he'd do. But it's nearly two weeks since he came. Doesn't bring back what he's got. Doesn't pick up what we got ready for him."

"If he doesn't come today, I suppose I'd better telephone . . . ?" said Lucia.

"Better had, ma'am," said Sibyl.

She drank a cup of coffee in the kitchen, waiting, very restless, for old Mr. Harper to come down. She was waiting for him in the hall.

"Father," she said, "you know that man who came to the boathouse night before last . . . ? I thought I'd better tell you something about him."

"No need to, m'dear. Not unless he comes again, and I don't think that's likely. No, I don't think he'll be back in a hurry. I sent him——"

"Yes, I know you did, Father. His name is Stanley Schmidt."

"Schmidt, eh! German name."

"He is a German. He's a very queer, shady sort of man, Father, and I shouldn't like it ever to get known that Bee had had anything to do with him."

"What d'you mean, Lucia? How is he—shady?"

"I think he's a Nazi agent," said Lucia, readily.

"What! What! Then he ought to be reported."

"I did. I sent an anonymous letter to the F.B.I.," said Lucia. "Only you can see that we can't possibly let Bee get involved in this."

"No. No, of course not. Have you told her your opinion of the fellow, Lucia?"

"I thought it was better not to," said Lucia in a special tone, quiet, very significant.

It was a tone she had used on Tom, too. It implied that she and she alone could understand the mystery of a young girl's heart. It had always made Tom uneasy and it had the same effect now upon old Mr. Harper.

"Well . . . I dare say you know best," he said.

David came down now, followed a few minutes later by his sister. They all sat at the table together; a steady breeze blew in at the open windows; the sun made the glass and silver twinkle. Lucia glanced at her father's silvery hair, Bee's soft fair mane, David's sandy hair, rough on his stubborn skull. Let them alone! she cried in her heart. Let them *alone!*

"Here comes the postman!" said David, pushing back his chair. "Let's see if there's anything from Dad."

He went out, letting the swing door bang behind him, and came back with the mail.

"Four," he announced. "Two for you, Mother, and one for Bee, and one for me. V-mails. Newspaper for Grandpa and a letter for Sibyl, and some bills and stuff."

He and Bee opened their letters at once, but Lucia kept hers to read when she was alone. Old Mr. Harper opened his New York paper.

"Fair and warmer," he read. "High time, too. Most unseasonable weather we've been having. Let's see now . . . Things look very promising in Europe. Here's Monty . . . A good man . . . What's this? Ha! Body of Slain Art Dealer found on Simm's Island."

"Go on!" said David, looking up.

" 'The Horton County police report the discovery yesterday in an isolated swamp on Simm's Island of the body of Ted Darby, 34, whose name——' "

"Give it to me!" cried Bee.

"What?" said Mr. Harper.

"Give it to me!" she cried again.

"I want to read it," he began, but she snatched it out of his hand, and ran out of the room and up the stairs.

"What's the matter with her?" asked Mr. Harper.

"Probably someone she's heard of," said David. "She knows a lot of those arty people."

"She needn't have snatched the paper out of my hands," said Mr. Harper.

"She'll have a fine time now," said David. "She'll call up all the girls she knows. My *dear!* Have you *heard* about What's-his-name?"

"Nevertheless," said Mr. Harper, "she could have waited a few moments."

"Oh, you know how girls are with a nice juicy bit of gossip," said David, man to man.

Does he know anything? Lucia thought. Or is he just being loyal to Bee?

She did not permit herself to show any impatience or haste, but as soon as breakfast was finished, she went upstairs and knocked on Bee's door.

"It's me, Bee. Let me in, dear."

The key turned in the lock and Bee opened the door.

"Well, you win," she said, with that square, scornful smile.

Lucia went in, closing the door after her.

"I don't want to 'win,'" she said. "It's just—"

"You have won, though," said Bee. "I'm finished."

"Bee, you're *not!* Anyone can make a mistake."

"Not quite such a big mistake. I suppose what they've got in the paper is true . . . !"

"I haven't seen it yet."

"He was arrested, just before the war. He had some sort of little art gallery, where he sold obscene pictures. The police locked up the gallery but somehow he got into it before the trial, and daubed all over the pictures. Amusing, isn't it? What's more, he's already been divorced once, and his first wife accused him of swindling her out of all her money. I suppose you knew all this."

"No, I didn't, Bee. I didn't know anything about him."

"Then how did you know he was so—awful?"

"But when I saw him, Bee, I knew."

"How?"

"Well, I did . . ." said Lucia.

"But *how?* I saw a lot of Ted, and I'd never have thought he was—like that. I mean, he was so gay, and he seemed to be so careless. Not like anyone who'd plot things . . .

Mother, I'd like to know how *you*—caught on to him when *I* didn't?"

"But, Bee, I'm so much older——"

"But you've never been anywhere. You've never seen anything of life."

"That's rather silly, Bee. I'm married and I have two children."

"That's nothing," said Bee. "You told me how you met Daddy when you were still in school. I don't suppose you ever even *thought* of another man. You got engaged at seventeen."

"You're only seventeen yourself," said Lucia.

"It's a different era. Girls are different. They're not brought up in that sheltered way." She paused. "I want to get away," she said.

"What d'you mean, Bee?"

"I couldn't *stand* staying here!" Bee cried. "I don't want to see anybody I know. I'm never going back to that art school."

"Bee, you didn't tell anyone about Ted, did you?"

"Oh, not by name. But everyone knew I had a beau . . . I used to mention places we'd been—things like that. God! If anyone ever finds out that I fell for someone like Ted, I'll—I don't know. I'd rather be *dead.*"

"Don't say that, Bee."

"That happens to be exactly how I feel. God!"

"Bee, don't swear, dear."

"Oh, what does it matter? When I think that I let him kiss me—*lots* of times . . . I tell you I'd rather be *dead,* than have people know that."

Her blue eyes looked dark, in her face that was white

as paper. She was stung to desperation by this pain, this shame.

"I want to get *away!*" she said.

"Bee," said Lucia. "Bee, darling, the only way to stand things is to face them, take the consequences . . ."

"You're talking like *Grandpa!*"

I feel like him, thought Lucia.

"I suppose you've told Grandpa about Ted?"

"I haven't told anyone. I never intend to. You ought to know that, Bee."

"Well, I don't! I don't know *what* your ideas might be. You might think it was your 'duty' to tell Grandpa and Daddy. To teach me a lesson, or something."

"If you can think that . . ." said Lucia.

"I know you always do what you think is *best* for me," said Bee. "But you don't understand me."

Lucia said nothing.

"Will you help me to get away?" Bee demanded.

"Yes," said Lucia. "Let me see the paper, will you, Bee?"

"You'll help me to get away—at once?"

"Yes. We'll talk it over later. I'd like to see the paper, Bee."

She took it into her own room, and sat down on the edge of the unmade bed. The details of Ted Darby's past did not interest her. She was looking for something else.

The body was discovered yesterday afternoon by Henry Peters, 42, electrician, of Rockview, Conn. While walking along the shore, Mr. Peters was led, by the insistent barking of his dog, to enter the marsh . . .

Lieutenant Levy, of the Horton County police, stated the death had been caused by a wound in the throat with some pointed instrument, from twenty-four to thirty-six hours previous to the discovery. The police are following several clues.

What clues? Lucia thought. If they trace it back to me, back to Father, then nothing could save Bee. And those letters . . . ? Those letters! If I could somehow raise five thousand dollars . . . But there'd be nothing to stop him from asking for more, later on. He could hold back some of the letters. I wouldn't know.

She left the paper on the bed and went over to the window. Maybe that was Lieutenant Levy I saw this morning in the launch, she thought. He looked rather nice. Suppose I go to him and tell him the whole thing? After all, none of us has done anything criminal. It was probably illegal to take Ted away like that, but I wasn't covering up a crime, just an accident. It would be dreadfully hard on Father, but he can take it.

Only not Bee. She had a vision of Bee, standing up in a court, looking so tough and scornful. But, at heart, so desperate and wretched. Miss Holley, you had asked this man to meet you in the boathouse? You had visited this man in his hotel?

No! Lucia said to herself. I don't want Bee to face things, and take the consequence of things. I'm going to get her away somewhere. Angela, in Montreal? Unless you have to have papers to go to Canada in wartime . . . Well, then, there's Gracie's camp in Maine. I could telephone Gracie, right now.

Only she couldn't. Her father might hear her telephoning, or David might. No privacy was possible for her. It never had been, she thought, wondering. All my life, people have known everything I did, everywhere I went. I don't mean that anyone's ever been snooping or suspicious, it's just that somehow I've always lived in such a sort of public way, right out in the open.

I'll go into the village and telephone from the drugstore, she thought. I'll——

Sibyl was coming up the stairs, creaking, sighing a little. Reluctant to speak to anyone, Lucia hurried to the bathroom, to hide in there, but the door was locked.

"Just a moment!" said Bee, in a loud, choked voice.

Lucia hurried out into the hall.

"I think I'll do a little weeding," she said to Sibyl.

"Yes, ma'am," said Sibyl.

Gardening had no appeal for Lucia. She did it because it was a duty to have a victory garden. She put on a big burnt-straw hat and her heavy gloves. She took up the basket with shears and trowel, and went out of the back door to the patch the local gardener had dug and planted for her.

She was not at all sure which sprouting things were weeds. It's queer, she thought. Father and Bee and David all take it for granted I know what I'm doing. Only Sibyl knows better. There was another implement in the basket, a stubby little rakelike tool with curved prongs. She did not know the name of it, or its purpose, but it was her favorite. You couldn't do much harm with this, she thought, kneeling in the hot sun and scratching gently at the earth.

Mr. Donnelly can stop at the drugstore, she thought. I'll pop in and telephone to Gracie and arrange for Bee to go there at once. I'll tell Father and David that Gracie suddenly needed another counselor. Sibyl can do up a couple of wash dresses for Bee, and she can take my little gray coat for the train. We can send the other things after her. I've got enough cash.

"Mother . . ." said David.

She looked up at him and saw him frowning.

"There's a man who calls himself Donnelly," he said. "Says he's come to take you out for a drive."

"Well, yes," said Lucia, rising.

"You mean you're going out for a drive *alone* with him?"

"Why not?" said Lucia. "He was here to tea yesterday."

"So I heard," said David. "Well, suit yourself. But I think it's a mistake."

There was no time to argue with David now. Lucia ran upstairs to wash and change her dress. A hat, she thought; it looks better, and she put on the new hat Bee had persuaded her to buy in New York, a sort of sailor with an edging of white eyelet embroidery on the brim. She put on white gloves, too, glancing in the mirror. It seemed to her that she looked altogether correct and dignified.

"What time for lunch, ma'am?" Sibyl asked as she reached the lower hall.

"Oh . . . one o'clock as usual, Sibyl," Lucia answered. "I shan't be gone long."

I'm just going to take a little drive with a blackmailer, she thought. It's—hard to believe.

Donnelly was standing in the driveway, with one foot on the running board of a superb roadster. He was wearing a dark gray flannel jacket and slacks of a lighter gray. He looked handsome, aloof, and distinguished.

"Good morning!" Lucia said.

"Good morning," he answered, not smiling, and helped her into the car.

He drove off, down to the highway, with nonchalant skill.

"Would you mind stopping at the drugstore?" she asked.

"We can't use our car until we get the next coupons; and things pile up so."

"Certainly. If you'll call the turns . . . ?"

"Next turn right," she said, "and then straight ahead."

Isn't he even nervous? she thought. Doing a thing like this—a crime that could send him to prison for years? Isn't he the least bit ashamed? When they reached the village, she caught a glimpse of them in the plate-glass window of the furniture store, and it was astonishing. The big, well-dressed, well-groomed man, and beside him a lady with gloves and a stylish hat. Nobody would *believe* it, she thought.

"There's the drugstore, on the corner," she said. "I'll only be a minute."

She was mistaken. It took a long time to get the camp in Maine, and it took still longer to get Gracie Matthews, the proprietor.

"I *think* Miss Matthews is out on the lake," said the polished, anxious voice that answered the telephone. "I'll send after her."

It was hot in the booth and there was a very unpleasant smell. Lucia's hands grew damp, sweat came out on her forehead and her upper lip. Oh hurry up! Hurry up! she cried in her heart. I don't want to irritate him by making him wait so long.

Gracie, when at last she came, was very trying.

"Certainly, Lucia. I'd love to have the child. But not today. We couldn't meet the train. The station wagon's laid up. Say Monday."

"I'd like—she'd like to come today, Gracie."

"But what's the hurry, Lucia?"

"It just came into her head . . ."

"Well, tell her it'll be just as nice on Monday."

"Can't you arrange for tomorrow, Gracie?"

"Well, I could!" said Gracie. "But why? I'll have to arrange with the Camp Weelikeus people to pick her up at the station, and I don't like to do that if I can help it. We'll have our own station wagon on Monday, and I don't see *why* she can't wait till Monday. It's Friday already."

"You know how it is when you're young."

"I do not!" said Gracie, with her usual vigor. "When I was young, I didn't *expect* people to cater to my whims."

"Bee hasn't been too well. I don't think this climate——"

"If there's anything wrong with the child, don't send her here, Lucia. I've got thirty-eight girls and no trained nurse. I'm short two counselors."

"Bee would love to be a counselor, Gracie."

"She wouldn't do at all!" said Gracie. "She doesn't know anything about handling people. Too self-centered."

"She's not," said Lucia, mechanically. "Well, if you won't let her come tomorrow—"

"All right!" said Gracie. "Let her come. But it's only for *your* sake, Lucia. Personally, *I* wouldn't give in to an adolescent whim."

They spoke a little, about trains, about equipment.

"Two blankets," said Gracie. "A pillow. And—are you writing this down, Lucia?"

"Yes," said Lucia, lying without a qualm.

It was a long list.

"And if she has any hobbies, stamp album, scrapbook, knitting, water colors; anything like that, tell her to bring them along."

"I will, Gracie. I do appreciate this."

"I think you're very foolish," said Gracie, "to give in to your family the way you do. You can take my word for it, Lucia, that they'd think twice as much of you if you'd stand up to them."

"Maybe you're right," said Lucia. "But thanks ever so much, Gracie. I'll write."

She hung up the telephone and opened the door of the booth. I've been ages . . . she thought. And I didn't want to irritate him. He did not seem irritated. He got out politely and helped her into the car. He set off again through the village and along a tree-shaded road unfamiliar to her.

"Have you the money ready?" he asked.

"I couldn't," she said. "I couldn't get into town to the bank without everyone asking questions. I just want a little more time."

He drove on in silence for a way.

"Things are changed," he said, "with Darby dead."

"Yes," she said. "Yes, I suppose so."

"That makes it worse for the girl," he said.

"Not much," said Lucia, evenly. "It couldn't be."

"It will be worse," he said, "with all that will come out at the trial."

"What trial?"

"They will try the man who killed Darby," said Donnelly. "It was a good job he did, but they will try him."

"If they catch him."

"There's no great mystery in it, at all," said Donnelly. "There's a dozen people know the man."

Oh, no! Lucia thought. They can't. They *mustn't* arrest the wrong man.

"They could be mistaken," she said.

"You mean there are others would be glad to see him

out of the way?" he asked, and for the first time she saw him smile, a bleak and fleeting smile.

"Or it could have been an accident," she said.

He turned the car up a side road and slowed down.

"There's a roadhouse along here," he said. "It is a good one. Respectable. Would you have lunch with me there?"

"Oh, thank you," she said, startled. "But I've got to be home to lunch. I really ought to be getting home now."

"Any way you like it," he said, and backed the car down to the road. "Will you have the money tomorrow?" he asked.

"Monday," she said. "I can't do anything until Monday."

"I wouldn't be bothering you so," he said. "Only there's someone else in it."

"Someone else . . . ?"

"My partner," he said. "If it was me alone, I would drop the thing altogether. I would let you alone."

It's the oldest trick in the world, Lucia told herself, pretending to have a partner to blame things on.

"If I don't get the money," Donnelly went on, "he'll be out again after it."

"Again?" she asked. "You mean it's Nagle—Mr. Nagle?"

"You're quick," he said, glancing at her sidelong, and the blueness of his eyes surprised her.

"He's a horrible man," she said.

"Do you think so, now?" he asked. "He's been a good friend to me. It was him gave me my start when I first came over here."

"Did you come from the other side?"

"From Ireland," he said. "I had a great idea of this country, from all I'd heard. I ran away from home when I was fifteen, and I shipped as a cabin boy, the way I'd get here. But it took me near three years. I got here, right enough, on the first voyage, but the mate would not let me go ashore. He'd seen it in my eyes, maybe, that I was intending to jump ship. So there I was, standing on the deck, looking at the Statue of Liberty."

He fell silent, with the shadow of a smile on his face.

"Well, how did you get here?" Lucia asked.

"It would be tejus for you to hear," he said, modestly.

"I'd like to hear," she said.

That was true. She wanted to know what manner of man this was, so that she might deal with him better.

"Back we went, to Liverpool," he said. "I was down on the docks one day, looking for a ship would take me back here, when a stranger comes up, very civil. We talk for a while and then he says, 'Come and have a drink.' I was sixteen then, but I looked older. I never had had a drink and to tell you the truth, I was afraid of it, from all I'd heard. But I went along with him, to see what would come of it. The next I knew I was in a ship bound for Singapore. To China we went, to Japan. When we got back to Liverpool, my head was full of the wonders I'd seen, and I wanted more. I got another ship sailing east, Egypt, India . . ."

He was silent again for a time.

"It is a queer thing," he said. "When I'd the money to go traveling in style, I went back to those places. But they were not the same. Well . . . Maybe it was youth that was missing."

"But how did you get to New York?"

"There's no story to that," he said. "I saved my pay and bought a ticket."

And how did you get to be a blackmailer? she thought.

He must have been an adventurous and romantic boy, and how had he come to this?

"What did you do when you got here?" she asked.

"It's a thing you wouldn't believe," he said. "I knew I'd a cousin in Brooklyn. That's all I knew; no address, nothing at all but his name. I thought I could look him up, and off I went to Brooklyn, thinking it would be a small town. You wouldn't believe it . . . I walked up and down the streets, asking here and there: Did you ever hear of a Mr. Mulligan from County Clare? After a while I asked a policeman. There's a club near by, he says, for the men of County Clare. Go there, he says, and maybe you'll learn something. Well, my cousin was well known there. Someone took me out to the saloon he had, and my troubles were over, the first day I set foot in the country."

"Did you go to work for your cousin?" Lucia asked.

"No . . ." he said. "That wasn't quite the way of it. Y'see, he made book on the side——"

"What's that?"

"He took bets on the horse races," Donnelly explained. "He took me out to Belmont Park with him and I met a lot of his friends, and they'd put me on to one thing or another. Then I got in with the ward boss. I got in with everyone."

"But didn't you have a job? A regular job?"

"I did not," he said, with a certain pride. "I've never had a job in my life, since the three voyages I made."

"But didn't you ever want a regular job with a salary?"

"I did not," he said. "That's not in my nature."

And what is your nature? she thought. She could not understand him at all. She could not even imagine what his life had been, or what sort of world he lived in. He doesn't seem like a really *bad* man, she thought. Could I possibly talk him out of this?

But her own house was in sight now. There was no more time.

"I'll ask my partner will he wait till Monday," said Donnelly, "but I don't know . . . Are you sure you'll have it Monday?"

"Yes," said Lucia.

By Monday Bee would be gone. And I'll think of something . . . she told herself. Some way out of this.

When they turned into the drive, there was a high van drawn up before the house. Eagle Laundry. The driver was standing beside it, and Sibyl stood on the steps above him.

"Says he's only coming once a month," she said.

"A *month!*" cried Lucia. "But we can't possibly manage——"

"Best we can do," said the driver, a lean, dark young man in a visored cap. "Haven't got the gas, haven't got the tires, haven't got the men to make a pickup any oftener."

"I'll do it *myself,*" said Sibyl, with a sort of passion, "before I wait a *month.*"

"Okay!" said the driver and got back into his van.

He backed and turned and drove off. Donnelly got out and helped Lucia to descend.

"I'll get in touch with you," he said, standing hat in hand.

She was surprised to see him turn to Sibyl with a smile and a gesture like a salute.

Chapter Seven

What's the *idea?*" Bee demanded. "It's not *like* you, Mother, to go running around with that man."

"I'm not running around," said Lucia. "He wanted to show me an old house. Historic. We'd better make a list, Bee, of what you'll need. Aunt Gracie said blankets and a pillow."

"I can't carry all that," said Bee. "And there aren't any porters any more. Anyhow, Gracie's sure to have some spares, she's so damned efficient."

"Bee, don't swear. You know how Daddy hates it. And Aunt Gracie."

"She's not an aunt, thank God."

"She loves you and David to call her 'Aunt.'"

"We haven't, for years. Personally, I'm not crazy about her at all. I wouldn't go near her gruesome camp, if I didn't have to get away from here."

Lucia was sitting on the bed in Bee's room, and Bee stood before her, barefoot, in an ivory satin slip, so lovely, and so remote. How much did she care for Ted Darby? Lucia thought. How much does all this mean to her? I don't know. She's very nervous. She didn't eat anything for lunch. But is she sad about it?

I *ought* to know. I ought to be able to talk to my own child.

"David took me over to the Yacht Club this morning," Bee began.

"But how could he? We don't belong to it."

"He knows people there. He's rather good at making friends. There was rather a nice crowd there, not all kids, either. I'd have had a nice time there, only I kept thinking all the time. Suppose any of them ever heard about Ted and me. It makes me *hate* him."

"Bee! He's dead."

"I hate him!" said Bee. "I'll never forgive him for the harm he's done me."

"Bee, what harm, darling?"

"He's made it so I can never trust a man again."

"He hasn't, Bee. Just think of your father and Grandpa and David."

"You don't realize," said Bee, "how rare they are. You don't realize how lucky you've been. Your life may have been stodgy, but at least you've never been deceived and humiliated. What's that Donnelly man like?"

"Oh, he's very pleasant," said Lucia. "Now let's get out your list, Bee."

"He's good-looking," said Bee. "But *I* think he's a wolf."

"Well, it doesn't matter," said Lucia. "You'll take your flannel dressing gown, of course."

"The thing is, *you* wouldn't *know* if he was a wolf."

"Certainly I should. I'm not an idiot."

"Mother, did you *ever* have anyone proposition you?"

"I shouldn't tell you if I had," said Lucia.

"That's where you make a mistake," said Bee. "Pretending to be superhuman."

"I don't pretend to be superhuman."

"But you do. You wouldn't let anyone see you shed a single tear when Daddy left."

"Why should I let people see me if I'm not happy?"

"It would be a lot better if you did. If you weren't so darned inhibited, I could *talk* to you."

Oh, Bee! Can't you talk to me? Lucia cried in her heart. I want that so. I do understand things.

David was springing up the stairs.

"Mother," he said, from the hall. "Someone wants to see you."

His voice was ominous.

"Oh, who, David?"

"He says Mr. Donnelly sent him. I'll stick around," said David. "Keep an eye on the spoons. He's on the porch."

"Try on that brown skirt of mine, Bee," said Lucia. "I'll be right back."

"Mother, what goes on?" Bee demanded. "Who *is* this Donnelly man anyhow?"

"I told you," said Lucia. "I'll be back in a moment."

From a window in the sitting room, Lucia could see the man on the porch, and her heart sank. He was the worst yet, far the worst, the most obviously shady and suspect. He was young, a boy, in a dark red sweater clinging tight to his skinny torso; he had a rough mop of black hair, and small black eyes set too close to a broad nose.

I suppose there's a gang, she thought. A whole gang of blackmailers. They'll keep on and on . . . Well, the first thing is to get Bee away. Then I'll see. Then I'll think.

Cold with dismay, she opened the door and went out.

"You want to see me?" she asked.

"Yeah," said the boy. "Regal Snowdrop."

"What?" said Lucia.

"Regal Snowdrop," he replied, impatiently. "Mr. Donnelly tole me to come. To pick up your laundry."

"Oh . . . laundry?" she repeated.

"Yeah. Laundry."

She was silent, trying to understand. This must be a sort of code, she thought. He must have come to get money, or a check, or something. And suppose he won't go away without it?

"Mr. Donnelly said tomorrow," she said cautiously.

"Well, he tole us today. Said we got to make dis a special job. Pick it up today, bring it back Tuesday."

"You *mean* laundry?"

"Well, jeez, lady, didn't I *say?* Laundry. What gets washed and ironed. Laundry."

"Mr. Donnelly sent you?"

"He said youse was having problems."

"But how can you take it?"

"I got a car here," he said, jerking his head, and she saw, parked down the drive, a very shabby little blue coupé. "Listen!" he said. "I haven't got all night, lady."

"No," she said. "I'll get it for you."

She went into the house, a little dazed, into the kitchen to Sibyl.

"There's a boy here for the laundry," she said. "They're going to send it back Tuesday."

"It's a new laundry, ma'am?" asked Sibyl.

It seemed to Lucia that Sibyl was looking at her in an odd way.

"Yes," she answered, in a matter-of-fact way. "It's the Regal Snowdrop. If you'll give it to the boy, please, Sibyl."

David was waiting in the hall.

"What gives?" he asked briefly.

"Why, nothing," said Lucia. "It's simply a boy for the laundry."

"Why hasn't he got a van?"

"I don't know. I don't care, either."

"What's the Donnelly man got to do with our laundry?"

"He knew of this laundry, and he wanted to be obliging."

"He can oblige me by keeping away from here," said David.

"Don't be silly," said Lucia, mechanically, and went up the stairs to Bee.

"Who was it?" Bee asked.

"Oh, it was a boy for the laundry."

"How did Mr. Donnelly get into it?"

"He knew about the laundry, and sent the boy."

"Well, why?"

"Why *not?* I'm tired of all these questions!" cried Lucia.

"Mother!" said Bee, shocked. "I never saw you like this before."

"Like what?" Lucia asked coldly. "Turn around, Bee, and let me see how that skirt is in the back."

This won't do, she told herself. It's not like me to get so irritable. Only I'm—I don't know. I feel tired, I guess. But I've got to keep hold of myself or they'll all notice.

They were all dangerous to her, her father, her daughter and her son. And Sibyl? I don't know, she thought. But I've got to be let alone, to handle this thing. I've got to think it out carefully. I'll get Bee away. And I wish I could get Father away.

It seemed to her that if only she could hide them somewhere, in safety, she could cope with the growing menace of her problems. If they were away, I could think, she told herself, and knew in her heart that she had not been thinking, that she had no plans at all. Nothing but this quite useless, stupid impulse to put things off, to gain one more day from Donnelly and Nagle. I couldn't possibly get hold of five thousand dollars, she thought.

But if I have to?

No, it wouldn't do any good. Blackmailers never stop. They wouldn't give me back all the letters. I couldn't know. She was in her own room, sewing a sash on Bee's house coat, a sweet little house coat, of dusty pink rayon, faintly fragrant of perfume. It made her want to cry; she did begin to cry a little.

But that had to be stopped. Someone would come and see her. Someone always came. There was always a knock at the door. Everyone had a right to come to her; that was what she was for, that was her function, her reason for being. There was never an hour that belonged to her.

The knock came and it was Sibyl.

"Mr. Harper's got a man from the police downstairs, ma'am," she said. "He's asked him to stay to tea."

"From the police?" Lucia cried.

"Yes, ma'am," said Sibyl. "But I don't think there's anything to worry about. He came right to the back door and he spoke to me first. Says he's going to all the people in this neighborhood, got to see if anybody knew Mr. Darby."

Was that compassion in Sibyl's voice, and in her amber-flecked eyes? Did she know anything? Or everything? Don't ask her. Don't try to find out.

"Is—where's Miss Bee?" she asked.

"She went out walking with a young man, ma'am."

"*What* young man?"

"Only the neighbors, ma'am. Seems to be a *nice* young man," said Sibyl.

It was compassion in her voice, and understanding.

"A *nice* young man," she repeated.

"I'll go down," said Lucia.

"Yes, ma'am. Mr. Harper's pleased to have company for tea. He doesn't worry about the police, ma'am. Got nothing on his conscience."

So you know? Lucia thought. But she could not be sure, and she did not want to be. She washed, and brushed her hair, and put on a fresh dress, and hastened down to the sitting room.

"Oh, Lucia . . ." said her father. "This is Lieutenant Levy, from the Horton County police. Lieutenant, my daughter, Mrs. Holley."

The lieutenant had risen, a tall young man with big feet and big, rather outstanding ears. He was not in uniform; in a neat gray suit he was not formidable, his smile was friendly, his dark eyes were thoughtful and mild. But she was very greatly afraid of him.

"The lieutenant is making some routine inquiries," said Mr. Harper. "He's investigating a homicide."

That *you* committed, Lucia thought.

Chapter Eight

The postman came, while they were at tea, and there was a V-mail from Tom. Lucia kept it, unopened, in her hand. There was comfort in it, and in the thought of Tom, who was so definite about things, so uncomplicated. Here, I'll look after this, Lucia, he would say. And if he saw that she had dreadfully mismanaged things, he would not be angry, or reproachful, or impatient. I think you made a bit of a mistake right here, Lucia . . .

She was very thankful that Levy asked her no questions at all. He didn't even want to talk about Ted. But Mr. Harper did.

"I read about the case in the newspapers," he said. "Didn't mention it, because I didn't want to alarm you or Bee. Too near home, what? But it looks very like one of these gangster murders to me."

"Let's not talk about it," said Lucia suddenly, and more loudly than she meant.

"Certainly, m'dear. Certainly," said her father, instantly contrite.

It was as Sibyl had said, he was pleased to have company for tea. He's lonely, Lucia thought. He misses his office and his club. And he misses Tom so very much. They used to talk. He's lonely and he's getting old . . .

He was getting old in such a clean, fine way, his silver hair cropped close, his nails so neatly clipped, his necktie pressed that morning, a brown and a yellow check . . . I could cry, she thought, and was shocked at herself.

Levy asked her if she had read a certain book very popular just then.

"Well, no," she answered. "Have you?"

He had, and he talked a little about it. He's not—right, she thought. He's not like a policeman. Suppose he really isn't one? Suppose he's someone that Nagle sent?

Her home was invaded, it was no longer a safe refuge for her people. If I could only put Father on his guard somehow, she thought, so that he wouldn't say anything . . . But maybe he had already 'said something,' had, in his innocence, completely betrayed himself?

She looked and looked at Levy, trying to read his face. In vain. He looked mild, a little sad, nothing more. If he was a policeman, why did he stay and stay and stay, like this? To trap someone.

He stayed and stayed, and Bee came home. She brought a boy with her, and he seemed to Lucia a sinister boy, dark and unsmiling; his shoulders were too broad, he looked powerful and aggressive.

"Mother," Bee said, "this is Owen Lloyd."

Owen took her outstretched hand in a grip that made her wince. He then shook hands in turn with Mr. Harper and Lieutenant Levy.

"You're looking into that case over on the island, sir?" he asked Levy. "This Darby?"

Lucia was stricken with terror to see how white Bee grew. If Levy looked at her *now* . . . she thought.

"Oh, we have our routine," Levy answered. "We're visiting everyone in the neighborhood, to see if we can pick up any information."

"My mother'll give you plenty, sir," said Owen. "She's been wanting to go to the police with her story. She says that early Wednesday morning she looked out of her window, and she saw a man and a woman, standing up in a motorboat between here and the island. Struggling, she says they were. She turned away to get her glasses and when she found them, and looked again, the man had disappeared, and the woman was heading for the island."

"Why didn't your mother come to us, Mr. Lloyd?"

"My father and I put her off it," said Lloyd. "We thought maybe she was mistaken, and she'd get herself all upset for nothing. She's pretty high-strung, you know."

"I see!" said Levy.

He finished his second cup of tea and rose.

"Thanks very much, Mrs. Holley," he said. "It's been very enjoyable."

"Stop in again, sir," said old Mr. Harper. "I'd be very interested to hear anything about this case you feel at liberty to tell."

"I will, Mr. Harper!" said Levy, earnestly.

Now it was the boy Owen who stayed and stayed, and Lucia stayed, too, until her father left to take his before-dinner stroll. Then she went up to her own room, longing for the solace of Tom's letter.

But it was one of his queer letters, filled with an almost wild hilarity. She had had two or three others like this and they had disturbed her profoundly. Tom never drinks too much, she thought. It's not that. Is it battle that makes him so excited?

She tried to think of her good-humored, nonchalant Tom

in battle. She recalled the battles she had seen in newsreels. Flames, smoke, hideous noises, whining, droning, screaming, shattering crashes. I can't . . . she thought. It's no use. He's too far away . . .

She sat on a chest by the window, in a curious apathy, until David came knocking at the door.

"Sibyl says you got a letter from Dad," he said. "What does he say?"

"Why, nothing very special, dear," she said. "Of course he's not able to tell anything much."

"Owen was in the Pacific zone," David said.

He glanced at Lucia, frowning a little.

"Well, if it isn't over pretty soon," he said, "it'll be my turn."

He had never spoken of that before, he said it now as if it were a question, as if he were asking her, what is this? What shall I think about life and war and death?

He looked so young, so slight. No! she said in her heart. *No!*

And who was she saying that to? She had no power to protect her own people, her own children. The walls of her home were falling down; there was no refuge.

"Have you got a clean shirt for dinner, dear?" she asked. "Give that one to me when you take it off. The collar . . ." She touched the collar at the back of his thin young neck. "It's a little frayed . . ."

"Oh, all right," he said with a sigh and went away disappointed.

Chapter Nine

Lucia sat up in bed to read over the letter she had written the night before.

DEAR TOM:

Bee is going to Gracie's camp for a week or two. I think it will do her good. It really is pretty dull here.

Dull . . . she repeated to herself, but she let it stand.

You ask how the car is standing up. We scarcely ever use it on account of tires and gas, so it will be in nice shape when you get back. I told Sibyl you sent her your best regards and she said to tell you she prays for you every night. She *means* it, too, Tom. I don't know what I'd do without Sibyl.

She leaned back against the pillows, thinking of Sibyl and what she might know. It was a sparkling morning, but she had no thought of going out. She had to stay here, right here, inside the house, so that nothing could happen. I will stop things, too, she told herself. I don't know now just what I'll do, but as they come up . . .

Nagle and Donnelly and Levy . . . Five thousand dollars . . . My jewelry! she thought suddenly. She had her diamond engagement ring, an emerald ring her father had given her on her twenty-first birthday, a string of pearls her mother had left her, her grandmother's diamond bracelet, all in the safe-deposit box in the New York bank. I could borrow on them, she thought. Or if it comes to the worst, I could even sell them.

To pay blackmail? Yes, she thought. It may be terribly stupid, but that's what I'm going to do. It'll keep those men quiet for a while, anyhow. It'll gain time.

And time must be her ally. She clung to that belief. She lived by it, now. Every day made the end of the war nearer, every day that no telegram came about Tom was a day gained. She lived as if holding her breath. Just get through this day.

She got a book and read it in bed, with stubborn determination. It was a mystery story she had got out of the lending library for her father, and she was not fond of mystery stories. Nobody in them ever seems to feel *sorry* about murders, she had said. They're presented as a problem, m'dear, her father said. What's more, they generally show the murdered person as someone you can't waste any pity on. *I'm* sorry for them, she said, I hate it when they're found with daggers sticking in them and their eyes all staring from poison and things like that.

Yet how little pity did she feel for Ted Darby! I really did that, she thought amazed. I concealed a body. Anyhow I took it away. And when I came back—after that—nobody could see anything wrong with me—anything queer. Maybe I haven't got so much feeling, after all. Maybe I'm rather too tough.

I'd better be, too, she thought, as she rose and began to dress.

Breakfast that morning had an unusual quality. She was surprised to find all her family so cheerful and talkative. Surprised but not pleased; it worried her. They were too innocent. They seemed this morning like victims, pitiably unaware of what darkly menaced them.

She saw the menace more vividly now than ever before. Her father standing in the dock. My dear, I don't like to be hurried, she'd heard him say all her life. But, once accused, he could be hurried. Question after question would be shot at him. She pictured him growing a little confused, indignant. She could imagine his overwhelming shame when he heard of Bee's folly. He and David. Tom would be different, she thought. He'd just be so sorry for Bee.

"Owen's mother wants to call on you," said David.

"Owen? Owen?" said Mr. Harper. "Oh, yes! Nice lad."

"He's twenty-three," said David. "And he was in the Army two years."

"His mother's a frightful nitwit," said Bee. "But she's rather nice. They're quite a nice family."

"Rolling in money," said David, complacently. "Absolutely rolling. I found them."

"Oh, you're a marvel!" said Bee, with scornful good humor.

"I know the art of making friends," said David. "Mother, the Lloyds asked me to lunch today. That all right with you?"

"Perfectly, dear," said Lucia. "Have you got a clean shirt?"

She went into the kitchen to consult with Sibyl.

"If that icebox man doesn't come today," said Sibyl. "I don't know how we're going to keep a thing over Sunday."

They stood in gloomy silence for a moment.

"I'd better get to market early," said Sibyl. "Better leave everything and get the nine o'clock bus."

"I'll do the marketing, Sibyl."

"No, ma'am," said Sibyl. "Better for me to do it Saturday. I'll go early and get back in time to iron those little things for Miss Bee." She thought for a time. "Best give me twenty dollars, ma'am."

"I'll send for a taxi," Lucia said. "And you'd better keep it, Sibyl. I'll pay it by the hour."

Bee wanted to go to the village, too; she and Sibyl set off in the cab. David had gone already; old Mr. Harper was taking his walk. Lucia put on an apron and was starting to wash the breakfast dishes when the telephone rang. She dried her hands and went to answer.

"Mrs. Holley, please," said a man's muffled voice.

"This is me," said Lucia.

"Donnelly speaking. I'd like to see you this morning for a few moments, Mrs. Holley. What time could I come?"

"Oh . . . !" she cried. "I'm afraid . . . You'd really better not come *here*."

"Well, I must see you somewhere, then."

"I don't know . . . I don't see . . ."

"Down at the railroad station, maybe. I am there now."

"I couldn't. I couldn't get away."

"I am sorry to bother you," he said.

"Can't you tell me what it is on the telephone?"

"It is not a good thing to be talking too much on the telephone," he said.

"I don't see *how* I can meet you *anywhere*."

"It is important," he said. "Else I shouldn't be bothering you. Is there someplace maybe near by where you can see me for a moment?"

"Wait," she said. "Let me think . . . There's the boathouse here. If you go by the shore road and then along a little path, you can get into it without anyone seeing you."

"What time will I be there?"

"Oh . . . It's very hard for me to say . . . I mean, I'll have to wait for a chance to slip out."

"I'll go there now," he said, "and I'll wait."

"Wait upstairs, please," she said. "I'll try to come right away, but I *might* be delayed."

"Don't worry," he said. "I'll wait."

She hung up the telephone and stood beside it, irresolute, flustered. There are such a lot of things . . . she thought. People are *idiots* to talk about getting married and being your own mistress, so much more free than women with jobs.

If Bee comes back and finds the dishes in the sink . . . Even unsuspicious Father would think that was queer . . . What reason can I give anyone for running out of the house?

"Oh, I don't know!" she cried aloud in angry desperation. "It's nobody's business."

She decided to finish washing the dishes, and leave them draining. Then I'll tell them, if they ask me, that I felt like being alone. I'll say I wanted to *think*. Why shouldn't I? Other people do.

She ran upstairs to powder her face and her anger increased, to see herself flushed and disheveled. Anger at them, her father, her children, and Sibyl. It's none of their business if I feel like leaving the house for a few moments. And the beds not made . . . I've got to make Father's bed. He's so neat. He'd hate to come back and find it not done.

Bee ought to make her own bed. Oh, Bee, my darling . . . ! Nagle and Mr. Donnelly, and maybe other people, horrible people, reading your poor silly letters. Trying to make money out of them . . .

This afternoon Bee would be going away, perhaps for weeks. Perhaps this trouble couldn't be kept away from her. I've got to make her bed, Lucia thought. Or she'd think I didn't love her.

She could not stop. She made David's bed too. She picked up, she tidied up the bathroom. David had left a ring in the tub. She took up the scouring powder and the rag. No! she told herself. I've got to see Mr. Donnelly and hear whatever it is. This is silly.

But she had to clean the tub. She ran down the stairs, and she nearly cried, because she wanted so terribly to empty the ash trays and straighten up the sitting room. She ran across the lawn and into the cottage part of the boathouse, hot, angry, miserable.

She went through the sitting room on the ground floor and up the stairs, and Donnelly stood on the landing waiting for her.

"I'm sorry I kept you waiting," she said briefly. "But I was very busy this morning."

"You hurried too much," he said. "You're out of breath and all. I did not mind waiting."

"Well . . . Let's go in here," she said, and led the way into one of the two bedrooms, a big room, dimly lit through the grimy windows, with two sagging couches against the wall, everything covered thick with dust.

Lucia sat down in a rocking chair with a torn and discolored antimacassar on the back, and Donnelly stood before her.

"Why is it the ladies don't carry fans any more?" he asked.

"Well, I don't think I ever did," Lucia answered.

"No. You're too young. I remember a long time ago, I

was in New Orleans and there was a girl there, French, she was, and dark like yourself, and she'd a little fan, purple, maybe. I don't know the names of those pretty, light colors."

He was trying to give her time to grow calmer, and she responded courteously,

"There's mauve," she said, "and lavender and violet."

"They are pretty names."

There was a silence. She rocked and the floor boards squeaked. Donnelly stood before her, arms at his sides, his head averted, immaculate and elegant in his dark suit and handsome olive-green tie.

"I am sorry this ever began at all," he said. "If I was in it alone, I'd hand you the letters and you'd hear no more about it."

"Well . . ." she said with a sigh.

"I told Nagle you said give you till Monday. He did not like that. It was all I could do to keep him from coming here himself."

"That wouldn't do him any good. It would only make things worse."

"That's what he wants. He wants to keep after you till you'll be desperate and get the money one way or another."

"But not *you*, of course!" she cried.

"Not me," he said.

A great anger was rising in her against Donnelly. He's a crook, she thought, and probably a very smart one. He's trying to trap me in some way. He's trying to deceive me. He's—I don't know what he's trying to do but it's something horrible.

"So Mr. Nagle's to blame for *all* of this?" she said, with a faint smile.

"Well, no . . ." Donnelly said. "No. I couldn't say that. When he first brought it up, I didn't make any objections."

"But now you've changed. You've got very high-minded about it."

"Now I wish to God I could stop it all," he said. "Only I cannot. Nagle is a man hard to handle. There'll be money coming to us from this deal we made. But things are bad now for the two of us, and he is nervous. He likes to have a bit of ready cash by him, in case anything'll be going wrong."

"But not *you*. *You* don't want this money, this blackmail!"

"I do not," he said. "Only I cannot hold Nagle off longer than Monday. Are you sure you can get the money that day?"

"Yes," she said carelessly, recklessly.

Bee would get away this afternoon, and there would be all Sunday to think things over, to make a plan.

"Will I come out here to get it?" he asked. "Or would you rather meet me in New York?"

"I'll meet you in New York," she said.

"When would it suit you?"

"I'll meet you outside Stern's on Forty-second Street," she said, "at noon."

She rose.

"There's one little thing more . . ." he said. "You'll only need bring forty-five hundred with you."

"Oh! How *nice* of Mr. Nagle!" she cried. "How kind and nice of him to let me off five hundred dollars!"

"I gave him five hundred," said Donnelly. "I told him

it was you sent it. I did that, the way he wouldn't be out here bothering you."

She looked straight into his face that was as it always was, handsome, strong boned, but blurred and veiled by something.

"I don't believe you," she said. "I don't believe any of this."

He said nothing and she went past him, out of the room and down the stairs. Liar! she cried to herself. Liar! I hate him!

She had never felt anything like this turmoil of the spirit, this anger. He's the one who brought the letters here. He's the one I'm to pay the blackmail to. And he says he did that. For me. Liar. Blackmailer. Contemptible crook. I hate him so . . .

She went back to the house, thinking of nothing but her anger. I will go to the police, she thought. I'll manage some way to keep Father out of it. The police will see to it that nobody ever knows anything about Bee's letters. They'll just arrest those men. That man!

She opened the front door and Bee came out of the sitting room. And at the sight of her child, all the other things rose in Lucia like a rushing tide. Getting Bee's clothes ready, packing, the lunch, the familiar feeling of things undone, things demanding attention.

"Oh, you're back, dear?" she said. "Did you get the things you wanted?"

"No," Bee answered. "But it doesn't matter. I'm not going to the camp, Mother. I sent Aunt Gracie a telegram."

"Bee! But why?"

Bee stood facing her, slight and lovely and curiously stern, all in white.

"I'm too much worried and upset about you," she said. "I'm shocked."

"What are you talking about?" cried Lucia.

"That man," Bee said. "The way you're acting with that man."

Chapter Ten

Lucia had felt irritated by her children now and then, and sometimes—not often—impatient. But this was anger.

"Don't talk like that," she said, curtly.

"How do you think I feel—we feel—David and I?"

"David would never be so silly and offensive."

"He feels just the way I do. When we found out that you'd sneaked out of the house to meet that man——"

"Don't say 'sneaked'!"

"You did! The moment we were gone——"

"I have things to talk over with Mr. Donnelly, and I'll see him when and where I think best."

"*What* things to talk over?"

"I certainly don't have to account to you," said Lucia. "And I'm not going to listen to any more of this. You'll have to go to the camp, as we arranged——"

"I'm not going. Not unless you promise me you won't see that man again. Ever."

"How can you dare to talk like that?" cried Lucia. "As if you had absolutely no confidence in your own mother."

"I met David in the village," said Bee, in a cold, even voice, "and that Halford kid gave us a lift home. You weren't in the house, and David thought maybe you'd taken out one of the boats. So we went to see. We thought we heard voices in the boathouse, and we opened the door——"

"You stood there listening!"

"We didn't. We came right out. We were absolutely shocked."

"Then you're both very silly—and offensive. I don't want to hear another word about this."

"David and I consider that we have an obligation to Daddy——"

"Shut up!" said Lucia, and went past Bee, into the house and up the stairs to her room.

I shouldn't have said that, she told herself. It was vulgar and horrible. Only, I don't care. My own children turning against me like that. I can't believe David would have ideas like that. I'm going to speak to him now, this instant.

But she did not move.

I can't speak to David about such a thing, she thought. About meeting a man. It's impossible. But David couldn't possibly think I was 'shocking.' Suppose I did step out to the boathouse to see Mr. Donnelly for a few moments, because I had things to talk over with him . . .

Then she remembered what it was that she had to talk over with Mr. Donnelly. Oh, no! she cried to herself. Let the children be shocked. Let them be exasperating, and offensive, anything at all. Anything was better than that they should know the truth. David would never get over it, she thought, if he knew that his sister had written letters like that to Ted Darby. And Bee would never, never get over it, if she knew that that Darby man didn't really care for her at all. That he was just planning to make money out of her.

I said I'd get the money by Monday, she thought. Mr.

Donnelly said that if I didn't, he couldn't keep Nagle from coming out here. I can't let that happen.

Then I'll have to get the money. Four thousand, five hundred dollars. I've got eight hundred, about, in my account now, and there'll be the allotment check and Mr. Fuller's check next month. But I have to pay the rent and the food and the storage on our furniture, and all the other things. My jewelry? I don't know how much it's worth. Thousands, maybe. But maybe not.

Those people who make loans . . . That's the thing! She remembered seeing advertisements in newspapers; she remembered hearing something on the radio. Privacy, they said. Your personal signature alone.

I know how stupid and wrong it is to pay money to blackmailers. But that's what I'm going to do. I want *time*. Time to get Bee away. Time for—other things. I don't know just what. Only, if I keep that Nagle man away, even for a while, there's a chance of something happening. He might have to run away. Mr. Donnelly said so.

A sort of fever possessed her. Her anger against Bee was forgotten; she was desperately impatient for Monday to come, so that she could get the money, and pay Nagle, and have peace. For a time.

There was a knock at the door.

"Who is it?" she called, with an unusual sharpness.

"Me," answered David's voice.

"Well, do you want anything special, David?" she asked. "I've got a headache."

"It's important," he said, and she opened the door.

"Now, if you're going to begin to nag, David——" she said.

"I'm not," he said. "I think you're making a big mistake,

taking up with that fellow, but I told Bee I was darn sure there was no real harm in it. Just folly."

His extreme calmness was as exasperating and as humiliating as Bee's shocked indignation.

"I'm not going to be talked to like this by a boy of fifteen," she said. "I know what I'm doing——"

"All right! All right!" he said, soothingly. "I came to tell you that Mrs. Lloyd's downstairs."

"Who is Mrs. Lloyd?"

"She's Owen's mother. She's got another son, around my age, and a daughter. They're nice people. They've got two cars and a chauffeur. They've got a swell cabin cruiser."

"What does she want?"

"Why, I suppose she just wants to see you," said David.

"I can't see her now. This time of the morning—and I'm not dressed."

"You look all right," said David. "Anyhow, she won't care."

"No, I can't!" said Lucia. "I'll—tell her I'll come to call on her."

"Mother, she's *right here!*" said David. "I can't tell her you won't come downstairs."

David was shocked now, and, in a way, he was not to be blamed. I'm being—very queer, Lucia thought.

She stopped being queer, at once.

"I'll be very glad to see your Mrs. Lloyd, dear," she said. "I'll be down in a minute."

Mrs. Lloyd was a thin woman, with rouge daubed carelessly on her hollow cheeks, and light hair in a thick, careless bun at the nape of her neck. She wore a white blouse too big for her, with cuffs that half covered her hands, and a bunchy gray skirt, and emerald-green wedgies. But she had a sweet voice, a sweet, triangular smile. Like a cat, Lucia thought. A mother cat, letting the kittens walk all over her.

"It's a *fearsome* time to come bothering you," she said. "But Owen and Phyllis and Nick got at me. I've been wanting to call—but really I never get around to anything." She paused. "I really don't know what I do all day," she said, with a sort of wonder.

"The days just go," said Lucia.

"Yes, *don't* they?" said Mrs. Lloyd. "Do you think you could possibly lunch with me at the Yacht Club some day soon? It's rather sweet there. You sit on the lawn—if it isn't *raining*, of course—and they bring little trays with fishes on them. *Painted* on them, I mean. A really very wonderful girl paints them. She supports her mother and her great-aunt in a tiny little cottage, and she paints simply anything. You send things to her, or she comes to the house. I didn't seem to have anything to send her, so I put her in our sun porch, and she painted simply adorable little fishes all over, on tables, you know, and on the walls. She does flowers, too, if you ask for them. And she did a simply huge horse's head for Mrs. Wynn, almost *too* huge, I thought, right over the mantelpiece. Do you paint, Mrs. Holley?"

"Why, no, I don't," Lucia answered, soothed and pleased by this most amiable guest.

"I don't, either, but I'd love to. Or play the piano, or something like that. When the children were little, they went to the Dame Nature School, and they played in a little orchestra. All the children did. It would be rather lovely if everyone kept *on* playing in orchestras, all their lives, don't you think? But do you think you could possibly come to lunch at the Yacht Club?"

"I'd love to," said Lucia.

"Tomorrow, perhaps? We could have their Sunday brunch. And David says your father is here with you. We should so love to have him—and there's a bar in the club-house. He'd like that, don't you think?"

"I'm sure he would," said Lucia.

"Then may we call by, tomorrow? The station wagon will hold us all. Twelve, do you think? I've tried to train myself to sleep late on Sunday mornings, but I can't do it. I seem to be so *hungry*. And then, it's rather charming, somehow, to go prowling around in the house, with everyone else asleep. Do you think I might ask that policeman to lunch with us? If you like him, that is."

"Well, what policeman?" asked Lucia.

"That Lieutenant Levy. I think he's so kind. And it would be nice to have another man. I'm so glad that really sinister case is settled, aren't you? That man on Simm's Island, I mean."

"Settled . . . ?" said Lucia.

"They've caught the murderer, and I'm *very* glad, because my Phyllis is only nineteen, and I do hate the thought of a murderer in the neighborhood."

"Do you know what man they've arrested?"

"I really know quite a lot about it," said Mrs. Lloyd. "We had Lieutenant Levy in for cocktails yesterday and he told us. It's a horrible man, named Murray. Underworld, you know. He was an enemy of that poor Darby man, and they came out here together on the same train. Imagine, in that teeming rain! I was rather surprised, because *I* thought he'd been killed by a woman."

"Oh! Did you?"

"Yes. Nick went over to the island, with another boy.

Boys that age seem strangely gruesome, don't you think? Nick found this list there, in the reeds."

"A list?"

"A market list. Quite pathetic, somehow. I mean, grated cheese, two points, and things like that. You simply felt sure it was a *nice* woman, not black market, of course, with those points all written down. I thought it was probably someone goaded to frenzy."

"That's very interesting," said Lucia. "I'd love to see the list, if you'd let me."

"But I gave it to Lieutenant Levy. It did seem to be a clue, don't you think?"

"Oh, I do!" said Lucia.

It must have been one of my lists, she thought. An old one. I must have pulled it out of my pocket with the bandanna. And Lieutenant Levy's got it. He'll know ways to trace it back to me; he'll know I was there.

But they arrested a man—after they'd got the list. So they can't think the list is very important.

"This Murray they've arrested . . ." she asked. "Is he a criminal?"

"Oh, heavens, yes!" said Mrs. Lloyd. "He'd just come out of another prison. He's a dope-peddler, and what untold harm they do, don't they?"

"Yes, they *do!*" said Lucia, earnestly.

"I was rather surprised," Mrs. Lloyd went on, "because I'd felt quite sure those two women had had something to do with it."

"What two women?"

"Oh, didn't I tell you? Well, you know, the morning the poor man was killed, I got up frightfully early, about half-past five, and I went out on my little balcony. And I saw a little motorboat, a little launch, like yours, you know, and two women were standing up in it, having a struggle."

But you didn't! Lucia thought. If there'd been another motorboat out, I'd have seen it. Certainly I'd have heard it. And there wasn't any. I could swear to that.

Mrs. Lloyd rose.

"I so look forward to our brunch tomorrow," she said. "You and your father and your two children. And shall I ask the policeman?"

"Oh, I think he's very nice," said Lucia.

David was not home to lunch, and Lucia sat at the table with her father and Bee, in a dream. It seemed to her that the world could offer nothing more desirable than Mrs. Lloyd's Sunday brunch. She had a remarkably clear vision of it in her mind; all of them sitting on a shady lawn, holding trays upon which fishes were painted, red and gold; Bee in her blue dress, she thought, and the sky pure blue, the calm sea a deeper blue. Father will enjoy it, she thought. And Bee . . . It's exactly the sort of thing Bee needs. There'll be Owen, and the daughter who's nineteen, and maybe other people will come. Maybe this is the beginning of a really happy summer for her.

"What did you think of Mrs. Lloyd?" Bee asked, with cold formality.

"I like her very much," said Lucia. "*Very* much. I don't know when I've met anyone I liked more."

"I don't think she's all that wonderful," said Bee, a little surprised, and still cold. "Of course, she's goodhearted and all that, but I think she's pretty silly. And irresponsible."

" 'Irresponsible'?" old Mr. Harper repeated. "That's a strong word, m'dear."

"Well, I mean muddled," said Bee. "For instance, one

time when I met her in the village, she asked me if I'd seen *Life with Father*. I said no, and she said she'd seen it just the week before, and she told me things out of it. But what she told me about wasn't *Life with Father* at all. It was a boring little play I'd seen with Sammy before we came out here."

"Well," said Mr. Harper, "considering the sort of plays they produce nowadays, I can't say that I blame the good lady."

"Honestly, Grandpa!" said Bee.

She always took him up on things like that; she began now to defend the theater of her own day, and old Mr. Harper was quite as ready to praise, and to describe, plays he had seen in London, in his boyhood. Lucia waited impatiently for the first pause.

"Mrs. Lloyd's asked us all to brunch with them tomorrow at the Yacht Club," she said. "She specially wants you, Father."

"Me?" he said, with a short laugh. He was pleased.

"I think it would be very nice," said Lucia.

"Well, they do know how to have a good time, the whole family," said Bee. "They're all popular, too. There's always a lot going on in their house, people coming and going and the telephone ringing."

"Ha . . . shouldn't care for that, myself," said Mr. Harper.

"I love it," said Bee. "This house is like a graveyard."

That's meant for me, thought Lucia. All right; I know I'm not popular.

"They're calling for us at twelve," she said.

Now it was done. She was letting Murray stay in prison.

Only over the week end, she told herself. I want Bee to

get a little established with the Lloyds. I want them to see what she's really like. Then, later on, if they hear anything —about Ted Darby, or anything else, they'll see . . . Just this brunch, and then I'll tell Lieutenant Levy.

That Murray has been in prison before. A few days won't seem so terrible, to him. He's a criminal, anyhow. Being a dope-peddler is as bad as being a murderer. It's murdering people's souls.

I mustn't talk that way to myself. Like a cheap movie. I don't know anything about Murray, except what Mrs. Lloyd said, and maybe she is a little—irresponsible. All I really know is, that he's in jail for something he didn't do. I could get him out. And I'm letting him stay there.

That's a sin, she said to herself.

A car was coming up the drive; someone was mounting the steps. It's the police, she thought. They've traced that market list.

"I'll go, Sibyl!" she called, and pushed back her chair.

A small delivery van stood outside the house and the driver, a burly man in a singlet, stood leaning against the porch rail.

"Holley?" he asked.

"Yes."

"Package," he said, and went back to the truck, returning with a big bundle clumsily wrapped in brown paper.

"Well, but from where?" Lucia asked.

"Wouldn't know," he said. "I was tole to deliver it to Mrs. Holley."

He held it out to her and she took it, and was surprised by its heaviness. The driver turned away, got into his truck, and drove off.

"What is it, Mother?" asked Bee, standing beside her.

"It's probably something Sibyl ordered," said Lucia. "I'll take it into the kitchen. Go on with your lunch."

But Bee followed her into the kitchen; she began to pick at the string on the package when Lucia set it down on the table.

"Why are you so inquisitive?" cried Lucia. "*Do* go back to your lunch, Bee!"

Sibyl stood by the window, silent.

"Good lord!" cried Bee. "It's a ham! A simply huge ham!"

"Came from my nephew," said Sibyl. "Told me he'd send one, soon as he could."

"Without any red points?" Bee demanded.

"I've got plenty of red points, Miss Bee," said Sibyl, mildly.

Bee followed her mother into the hall.

"I hope Sibyl isn't mixed up in any black market business," she said. "I *despise* that."

"You ought to know Sibyl better than that," said Lucia.

"Well, just the same, I call it very queer," said Bee. "A simply huge ham arriving, and nobody asking for red points, or money, or anything."

Lucia sat down at the table again. I don't know where that ham came from, she thought. And I'm not going to think about it. Ever.

Chapter Eleven

Dear Tom: We've met some very nice people here, named Lloyd. It was David who found them, of course; he's like you about making friends. Mrs. Lloyd's asked us all to brunch with them tomorrow at the Yacht Club, and it ought to be fun. Mrs. Lloyd says they serve lunch on little trays with fishes painted on them by a girl . . .

This is nonsense, she thought. How can I write drivel like this to Tom? Tom—in a war? But I don't know what to write to him. If he knew what I'd done . . . What I'm doing *now*. Letting an innocent man stay in prison.

It's a sin. What I did about Ted Darby was illegal. I dare say it was foolhardy. But this is a sin. It's bearing false witness against your neighbor, not to speak when you know the truth. Suppose Mrs. Lloyd is mistaken, and Murray isn't a criminal and a dope-peddler? Suppose he's a perfectly innocent man?

She had to get the letter finished, some sort of letter. But she was troubled by visions, very foreign to her. She imagined Tom standing on the deck of a ship that was rushing through the water; she could see his blunt-featured face raised to a sky sparkling with southern stars. She knew, in some way, that he was not thinking of her, but beyond that she could not go; she could not imagine the thoughts of a man with battle and death before him and behind him. She felt desolately remote from him, as never before.

That's because of what I've done, she thought. It's made a separation.

She took up her pen and finished the letter, fluently, quickly, and pointlessly. It was late, and she took a bath and got into bed, and turned out the light. And then she had visions of Murray. He was shaking the bars of his cell and shouting. Before God, I am innocent! I am an innocent man! His head was shaved and he was wearing a shapeless gray uniform. I am an innocent man! he cried. But nobody believed him.

Suppose he kills himself? she thought, and sat up in bed, aghast. The prisoner hanged himself in his cell last night. The prisoner cut his wrists. The prisoner went violently insane.

I'll have to tell Lieutenant Levy now, she thought. But I'll have to tell Father first. And then we'll get Lieutenant Levy on the telephone, and they'll let Murray out tonight.

She went along the hall to her father's room; she stood outside it, barefoot, in her pajamas, her black hair loose on her shoulders. Then she heard him cough a little, an elderly cough. A lonely cough. Did he lie awake in the nights, and think of his wife, who had lain beside him for twenty years? Did he think of the days when his life had been vigorous and stirring, and not lonely?

I won't do it! she said to herself. Not at this hour of the night. I won't do it.

And when she got back into bed again, she made up her mind that she would not do it until after that brunch. All right! she told herself. I'll take a chance. A chance that Murray won't get desperate. I'm gambling with a human life. That sounds like something out of a movie, but it's the truth.

On Sunday afternoon I'll tell Lieutenant Levy. No, I won't. On Monday morning I'll go to see that finance company, and if they won't lend me enough, I'll pawn my jewelry. I've got to get those letters back before the police get into this. It's going to be bad enough as it is, with all that shock and misery for Father. But I won't have Bee disgraced. I'm sorry about Murray. I'm so sorry . . .

Her visions of Murray so troubled her that she could not sleep; she got up and took two aspirins. You can see how people start taking drugs, she thought. Not from grief. I could bear it when Tom went away, when Mother died. It's this feeling of guilt, this horrible, shameful worry.

She waked later than usual; she dressed and went downstairs, and Sibyl was in the kitchen.

"Got the ham boiling," said Sibyl. "Then round about ten o'clock, I'll put it in the oven. Got some cloves left over, in a little jar. Got a little brown sugar. If you could spare a little sherry, ma'am?"

"Yes, of course," said Lucia.

She stood leaning against the doorway, heavy-eyed, oppressed. I suppose I ought to know . . . she thought. It's cowardly not to ask.

"Sibyl," she said. "Did your nephew really send that ham?"

"No, ma'am," Sibyl answered, without emphasis.

It seemed to Lucia necessary to go on with this.

"Well, have you any idea where it did come from, Sibyl?" she asked.

"No sense to look a gift horse in the mouth, ma'am," said Sibyl.

"Well, no . . ." said Lucia, and went into the dining room.

They took three newspapers on Sunday; one was especially for Mr. Harper; one had been requested by David, for certain comics he followed; the third was a sort of communal one. Lucia went through this one in haste, and found what she sought.

> The Horton County police have arrested Joseph 'Miami' Murray in connection with the slaying of Theodore Darby on Simm's Island. . . . Five years ago Darby figured in the news as a dealer in pornographic art. . . . 'Miami' Murray has twice been convicted on drug-peddling charges. . . .

It's like one of David's comic strips, she thought. They're so *very* criminal. Why should people like Father and Bee have to suffer, just to clear a man like that Murray?

She had learned that answer by the time she was ten years old. Because it was right to tell the truth, and wrong to hide it. Because it was wrong to let anyone be blamed, unjustly, for anything. It was as simple as that. *Thou shalt not bear false witness against thy neighbour.*

That drug-peddler isn't my 'neighbor'! she cried to herself. And I'm not bearing any kind of witness against him.

She could not eat anything. She drank the two cups of coffee from the little pot Sibyl had brought in, and then she went into the kitchen.

"Sibyl," she said, "I think I'd like another cup of coffee."

"Never knew you to take three, ma'am."

I never did, Lucia thought. I never wanted to. Only, today I want to be—nice. I want to be gay and pleasant. I want the Lloyds to think we're a nice family.

A nice family? she thought. When Father killed Ted Darby, and Bee wrote him those letters, and I took Ted to the island, and now I'm paying blackmail. Why, if anybody knew about us, we'd be—outcasts.

Nobody's going to know, she thought. I'm not going to think about that Murray any more today. I've made my decision, and I'll stick to it. And not think.

She was curiously undecided about what to wear for the brunch. It was a problem which, as a rule, concerned her very little, only now she felt sure of nothing. She did not even feel like Mrs. Holley.

I want to look nice, she thought. But not too formal. And thinking about this, she was inspired to remember a picture in a magazine, and that was how she wished to look. She put on a black blouse with a high neckline and a white skirt; she looked in the mirror and was pleased with the debonair and somehow soldierly effect.

Mr. Harper was waiting for her in the sitting room.

"I suppose," he said, "that as long as these people have invited me, I'd better go. But I'm a bit past the age for enjoying alfresco meals." He laughed a little. "I prefer my tea—without ants," he said.

Lucia laughed, too. Oh, you darling! she thought, with a pang. You're dying to go. And you look so nice and handsome and pleased.

"Are the children ready, do you think?" she asked.

"Oh, yes. Yes. On the veranda, reading the news," he said. "Quite a little family excursion, eh? All four of us."

He's proud of us, Lucia thought, and it touched her almost unbearably. Everything about this day had pain in it, and, with the pain, a feeling of reckless triumph. She had got this day for them; she had bought it for them, at a price she could not begin to compute. There could never be another day like it; it had, for her, the heartbreaking clarity of a lovely scene never to be revisited.

The Lloyds were bathed in this clear light. Mrs. Lloyd, her hair blowing wildly about her thin, rouged cheeks, sat among her children, with her sweet mother-cat smile, and they were gentle to her. There were Owen, and a vivid, pretty daughter, and a nimble boy of fourteen, all of them good-looking, polite, and at ease. More at ease, politer, gentler than David and Bee. Well, I dare say she's brought them up better, Lucia thought. But I do think David and Bee are more remarkable, somehow.

The brunch had style. A table was set ready for them on the terraced lawn overlooking the bright water; the chauffeur brought cocktails in a thermos jug.

"The bar doesn't open till one," Mrs. Lloyd explained. "And anyway, the ones you make at home are generally a little nicer, don't you think?"

"In this case, I agree with you," said Mr. Harper. "Smooth as velvet."

"I'm so *glad!*" said Mrs. Lloyd. "Lieutenant Levy doesn't seem to be here, does he? But he said he never could be sure."

" 'A policeman's lot is not a happy one,' " Mr. Harper quoted, and he and Mrs. Lloyd both laughed at that.

Lucia could have listened to them and watched them all for hours. It's the loveliest day . . . she told herself. David was talking, with amiable condescension, to the younger Lloyd boy; Bee and the daughter Phyllis were talking together. It interrupted her dreamlike pleasure when Owen sat down beside her and began to talk, with an obvious effort.

He talked about himself. He was, he said, going back to Harvard, to take his senior year, and then there would be a job waiting for him in New York.

"It's a pretty good job," he said. "It's only three thousand to start, but the possibilities are practically unlimited."

"Oh, that's nice!" said Lucia.

He went on and on, in a curiously boring way for someone so young. He told her about his fraternity, about his Army record, he told her about sailing trophies he had won. I must say he's rather egotistic, Lucia thought. And then, suddenly, it occurred to her that he was telling her these things for a reason. He was trying to explain his qualifications as a suitor of Bee's. Oh, no! Lucia thought, in a panic. Bee's only seventeen, and he's much too young, too. No! He mustn't——

"There's the Lieutenant!" said Phyllis Lloyd.

The brunch had been cleared away by this time, and they all strolled down to the beach, a mild and amiable herd. They scattered there, the young people went away; Mrs. Lloyd gave all her attention to Mr. Harper, and Levy sat on the sand beside Lucia. She did not want him there. His presence made her remember everything that she wanted to forget. She wanted this day to be an interlude, all sunny and clear, and Levy made her remember Murray, in prison.

He talked to her in his quiet and gentle way; he talked about sea gulls and snipe and sandpipers.

"What a lot you know about birds!" said Lucia, politely.

"Well, since I've come here, I've got interested," he said. "I'm making a study of the shore birds, taking photographs of them, and so on."

That's an attractive thing to do, Lucia thought. Too nice for a policeman.

"Do you *like* police work?" she asked.

"Not always," he answered. "I started out to be a lawyer, you know. I was admitted to the bar. But police work appeals to me more."

"I should think it would be horrible," said Lucia. "Hunting people down, trying to get them punished."

"The function of the police is protection, Mrs. Holley," he said. "It's not punitive. I have nothing to do with punishing anyone. I enforce the law, that's all."

"I don't think so much of 'the law,' " said Lucia. "I think it's often very stupid and unjust."

"It's all we have, Mrs. Holley," he said. "It's the only thing that can preserve anything at all of our civilization. Whether it's religious law, or civil law, as long as it's something we've all agreed upon, and something we all understand—in advance——"

"*I* don't understand the law," said Lucia.

"You made it, Mrs. Holley," he said. "If we have any laws of which you don't approve, you have the right to work for their repeal."

"Yes, I know," she said, secretly rebellious.

"Women, above all, should value government by law," he said. "It's the one protection you and your family have against aggressive and predatory people."

"Oh, yes, I'm sure you're quite right," said Lucia.

She did not like him when he talked about his precious law, and she stopped listening to him. She leaned back, with both palms flat on the sand, and she allowed herself to relax. Far down the beach she could see her children, with the young Lloyds and some others they had met; she could hear her father's voice, talking contentedly with Mrs. Lloyd. Nice friends for them to have, she thought. I'm very glad this happened, right now. It was an immeasurable comfort to her that it should be like this, a golden, tranquil day, friendly, and a little de luxe. No matter what happens to me, she thought, I'm pretty sure the Lloyds would stand by Bee and David and Father.

She believed that something was going to happen to her. She had no formed idea of what it would be; only it was as if, in a few hours, she was going to walk out of this sunny world into darkness. She was not frightened, simply resigned, and tired.

It's rather soothing to hear Lieutenant Levy droning on like this, she said to herself. I think he likes me. I'm sure he'd never suspect me of breaking any of his precious laws. He's—when you come to think of it, he talks like a grown-up David. Maybe David will be a lawyer. Or a policeman.

Then she realized that Levy had been silent for some time, and, like most shy people, she was afraid of silence. She glanced at him, and he was pouring sand through the open fingers of one hand, a fine, narrow hand; his head was bent, his face in profile was grave, even melancholy.

"I'd like to see a flamingo sometime," she said, anxiously. "They must be beautiful."

"They are," he said, looking up. "I've seen them, in Florida."

"Oh, you've been in Florida?"

"I went down there, after a man," he said. "However, I like our own birds better. Sandpipers . . . D'you often go over to Simm's Island, Mrs. Holley?"

"Why, no," she answered. "Only—once."

She hoped that this hesitation was not noticeable.

"We went there for a picnic," she went on, "but we didn't like it very much."

"Lots of sandpipers there," he said. "Did you find a fairly good place for your picnic, Mrs. Holley?"

"It was just a strip of beach."

"Most of the island is marshy," said Levy.

"Yes, it is," said Lucia.

"Still," he said, "there are a lot of inlets. It wouldn't be hard to get a boat well into the marshes."

She was afraid to look at him. A trap? she thought.

"But who'd want to?" she asked.

"To study the birds," he explained.

"Oh, yes!" said Lucia. "Yes, of course."

I don't think he means anything, she thought. I think he's too nice to want to trap me. Especially at a sort of little party like this. He's come here to relax and enjoy himself. Not as a policeman.

But he was a policeman.

He offered her a cigarette, and lit it for her and one for himself.

"My housekeeper's getting tough with me," he said, sadly. "She wants *me* to go to market for her."

"That's not right," said Lucia.

"She thinks I get preferential treatment," he said. "She tells me that whenever I take the list to the store, I get things she couldn't get."

"Well, it could be like that," said Lucia. "Someone in the police . . ."

"She says—let's hope it's not true, but she says they don't take enough points from me. Very unethical, that would be."

"I suppose it would be."

"For instance," he said, "how many points should I give for half a pound of Royal Grenadier cheese?"

"Twelve red points," said Lucia.

"Is it a good brand?"

"Oh, yes! We like it best of all."

He turned his head quickly.

"I see!" he said.

But he did not raise his eyes, to look at her. It was as if what he had heard was enough.

He did mean something. She had said something to make him prick up his ears.

Chapter Twelve

I've got to go in to New York this morning," Lucia said, at the breakfast table.

There was a silence; her family sat as if stunned.

"But, Mother! You never said a word . . . !" Bee protested.

"Well, why should I, dear?" said Lucia. "I've just got to run in, to look after some business."

"Business?" said her father. "I expect to be going in to town myself, later in the week. Maybe I could attend to things for you, m'dear."

"No, thank you, Father. It's just some little details."

There was another silence, and she resented it. Other people go to New York, she thought, and nobody's so amazed. I bet Mrs. Lloyd goes to New York whenever she feels like it. She made for herself a picture of Mrs. Lloyd at *her* breakfast table. Children, she said, I'm going in to New York this morning. Oh, are you, Mother? said her children.

"What train will you get back, Mother?" asked David.

"I don't know exactly, David. Early in the afternoon."

"If you'll make up your mind now," David said, "I'll meet you with the car."

"There's no sense wasting gas, when we're so short, David. I'll take a taxi."

"Very well," he said, stiffly.

"Mother," said Bee, "I think I'll go in with you."

"Well, not today, dear."

"I want to look at coats, little short coats. You can go ahead and attend to this 'business,' whatever it is, and I'll meet you for lunch."

"I'm having lunch," Lucia said, "with Mrs. Polk."

"For Pete's sake!" cried David. "What d'you want to see that old harpy for?"

Lucia regretted having chosen Mrs. Polk, a simpering white-haired lady of great culture, who had managed the lending library they had patronized in New York.

"You said she'd gone to Washington," said Bee.

Oh, let me alone! Lucia cried in her heart. Ask me no questions and I'll tell you no lies.

"Well, you wouldn't mind my being along, if it's only Mrs. Polk," said Bee.

"She said she wanted to talk to me about something rather special," said Lucia. "We'll go together someday very soon, Bee."

"But what could Mrs. Polk possibly want to talk to *you* about?" asked Bee. "You hardly know her."

"I wish you wouldn't keep *on* at me so!" cried Lucia. "I have absolutely no freedom at all! I can't do the simplest thing without all this nagging——"

She stopped short, well aware that she had shocked all of them, her father and her children. My disposition is getting horrible, she thought. Well, I'm sorry, but I can't help it.

"Will you telephone for a taxi, please, David?" she asked, with cold dignity.

All the way to the station, her anger occupied her mind.

Good heavens! Can't I even go in to town, without all this silly fuss? I'm not a child, or an idiot. I'm not a slave, either. I can go to New York whenever I think best, and I don't intend to be cross-examined by my own children. They ought to have confidence in me, and so should Father. Complete confidence.

But when she got on the train, she realized, with a faint shock, that what she ought to be doing, and must do, was to plan the day before her. First I'll go to the bank, she thought, and get my jewelry out of the safe-deposit. Then I'll go to that finance company. If I can't get enough from them, I'll have to pawn my things, to make up the difference. Anyhow, then I'll meet Mr. Donnelly and give him the money. Then I'll call up Lieutenant Levy. No. I'll have to warn Father first. Oh, how can I? How can I tell him he killed Ted Darby? They'll question him, and maybe they won't believe what he says.

They'll ask, why did you go to the boathouse to see deceased? I'll have to tell him not to mention Bee. I'll say I saw a light there, and I thought it was a prowler. That's a funny word, but everybody uses it. The lawn mower was taken by a prowler. There are prowlers in the neighborhood. I wonder if the police use it, write it down? John Doe, charged with prowling. I wonder if there are any women prowlers.

Stick to the point, you fool. Remember what this means. I could get Father to promise not to mention Bee, but I'd never, never be able to get him to tell a lie. He'd just be silent. Mr. Harper, why did you go to the boathouse? All by yourself, in the pouring rain? I refuse to answer that question, sir. Then we'll lock you up until you do answer.

Suppose they lock me up, too? For taking away the body. The children would be left alone. I know Sibyl would look after them, but think of the disgrace . . .

Oh, it can't be true! Things like this don't happen to people like us. I can't tell Lieutenant Levy. But I cannot let that Murray man stay in jail, not even one more night. Taking Ted away was breaking some sort of law, I suppose. But letting that Murray man stay in jail, when I know he's innocent, is really evil. It's a sin.

This was like a fever. Her thoughts came too fast; they merged one into another, in panic confusion. This won't do, she told herself. One thing at a time. First I've got to get the money, so that I can buy back poor little Bee's letters. That's the first thing. First things first. I can't afford to be so flustered.

When the train entered the tunnel, she looked at herself in the window, and she was dismayed. She had taken great pains with her dressing; a black suit, the little black hat with a veil, a white blouse, white gloves. Sophisticated, she had thought, and rather businesslike. But the image she saw in the black window looked idiotic; a white face, the collar of the blouse like a clown's ruffle, the little hat perching too high. Fool! she called herself. If I wasn't a fool, I wouldn't be in this position.

She took a taxi to the bank, and it was her misfortune that she kept on feeling like a fool, a clown. She felt that the man she spoke to was amazed at her and her request. Another man went with her, down to the strange, sinister vaults; a guard with a revolver in a holster opened the door for her and waited outside while she went in alone, to get out the jewelry. It was in a manila envelope, and on it was written, in Tom's handwriting, "Lucia's jewelry."

Oh, Tom! Oh, Tom! Everything so carefully arranged for me—so that there wouldn't be any trouble—if you didn't come back . . . A loud sob came, and a sudden rush of tears; she fought them furiously; she dried her eyes and came out.

The distinguished elderly man who had escorted her gave her a form to sign. "*Thank* you!" she said, and hurried away.

She took another taxi to the offices of the Individual Loan Service Association, and now she had no illusion left of seeming sophisticated and businesslike.

"You want to pay off on a loan?" a drowsy, dark-eyed boy asked her.

"I want to get a loan," she said. "Make a loan. I mean, get one."

"Aw right!" he said, and went away, leaving her in a stately high-ceilinged hall set with Renaissance furniture. A young woman came out, and led her to a table, a young woman with round, rouged cheeks and modishly waved white hair.

"What amount did you wish to borrow?" she asked.

"Oh . . . Five thousand dollars," Lucia answered.

"That's quite a lot of money," said the white-haired young woman. "Where are you employed, Mrs. . . . ?"

"Holley," said Lucia. "I'm not employed anywhere. Not just now."

"What is the purpose of this loan, Mrs. Holley?"

"Well, I need the money," said Lucia.

"Doctors' bills? Paying off a mortgage?"

"Well, your ad says, no red tape."

"We have to protect ourselves, Mrs. Holley. Especially

in the case of such a large amount. Have you a weekly or monthly income, Mrs. Holley?"

"Yes."

"What is the source of this income, Mrs. Holley?"

"It's from my husband."

"Will you give me the name and occupation of your husband, please?"

"I'd rather not," said Lucia. "You said you'd lend money on a note. All right. I'll sign a note."

"How much is your income, Mrs. Holley?"

"Well, it's around five hundred a month."

"How much do you think you could repay every month?"

"Well . . . Fifty dollars?"

"Do you realize how long it would take you to repay five thousand dollars at that rate, Mrs. Holley?"

"Yes!" said Lucia, loudly.

"I'm afraid we couldn't consider it, Mrs. Holley. Unless you have collateral. D'you own any property? A car?"

"I've got a car."

"In your own name?"

Tom did that. The car's in your name, Lucia, so that if you ever want to sell it, or trade it in, you won't have any trouble. So that if he didn't come back . . .

"What's the make of your car, Mrs. Holley? How old is it?"

She had to go on with this, but she had no hope left.

"Well, why don't you do this?" said the white-haired young woman. "Drive the car in someday, and we'll get someone to look it over. Ask for me. Miss Poser."

"Your ad said, no delay."

"But we have to protect ourselves, Mrs. Holley," said Miss Poser.

Against *me?* Lucia thought. As if I was a crook?

"Well, how much do you think they'd let me have on the car?" she asked.

Miss Poser said it depended upon the condition of the car, and upon other things.

"But what's the most I could get?" Lucia asked.

If everything was satisfactory, it might, Miss Poser said, come to five hundred dollars.

"Five *hundred!*" said Lucia.

Miss Poser rose.

"You drive the car around sometime," she said, pleasantly enough.

It was a dismissal. For the first time in her life, Lucia was a person to be got rid of, a queer, troublesome, suspect person. Coming around here, trying to get five thousand dollars. Did you ever!

"Would you like to see some jewelry?" Lucia asked.

"Why, no. No, thanks," said Miss Poser.

She was obviously startled and uneasy.

"We don't make loans on personal effects," she said.

"I see!" said Lucia. "Well, thanks!"

She went over to Madison Avenue and walked uptown, looking in vain for a pawnshop. It's getting late, she thought. Mr. Donnelly won't wait. He'll go away. She signaled a taxi and got into it.

"D'you know where there's a pawnshop?" she asked the driver. "A—reliable one?"

"Sure," said the driver.

She was glad that he showed no surprise, not even any interest. It probably doesn't seem queer to him, she thought. He probably knows about society women and duchesses and people like that pawning their jewels. Only Father'd be terribly upset. He has all those little jokes about hock shops, and cockneys hocking their Sunday clothes every Monday and getting them out on Saturday, and things like that. He'd hate me to be doing this.

I don't like it much, myself. But I don't care, if only they won't be rude to me. I didn't know I was so sensitive. It's rather disgusting, to be so sensitive. I thought I was pretty tough. But I'm not. Not when I get out in the world. Then I'm a nincompoop. If one of those reporters stopped me in the street and asked me what I thought about Russia, or something like that, he'd put me down as Mrs. Lucia Holley, Housewife.

Why is it 'housewife'? What would I call myself if we lived in a hotel? Nobody ever puts down just 'wife,' or even just 'mother.' If you haven't got a job, and you don't keep house, then you aren't anything, apparently. I wish I was something else. I mean, besides keeping house, I wish I was a designer, for instance. The children would think a lot more of me, if I was a designer. Maybe Tom would, too.

No! Tom likes me the way I am. Only, if I could be even a little different when he comes back? I don't mean bustling off to an office every morning. He wouldn't like that. But if I could go to an office or a store now and then, meet outside people. Have interesting little things to tell at dinner. Not be—just me, year after year . . .

"Here you are!" said the driver, stopping before a place on Sixth Avenue.

"Will you wait, please?" Lucia asked.

"Okay," said the driver.

She was frightened. It was such a queer little place, with a metal grille over the window in which was displayed a crazy jumble of things, a mandolin, clocks, candlesticks, a fur neckpiece, an old-fashioned pearl stickpin in a box lined with purple plush. Do they put everything in the window? she thought. I'd hate my things to be there. Mother's pearls, and the ring Tom gave me. I hate this! I hate all this! It's worse than taking Ted over to the island.

It was dim inside the shop, and so queer. A dark, moon-faced young man in shirt sleeves came behind the counter; she thought he looked scornful, and she put on a manner of cold aloofness.

"I'd like to borrow some money on some jewelry," she said.

He said nothing. She opened her purse and took out the long envelope; she handed him the little boxes and he emptied them onto the counter.

"How much do you want?" he asked.

"Well, as much as possible," said Lucia.

The rings, the bracelet, the clasps, the necklace lying on the counter looked, she thought, like junk, worthless and dull. He gathered them up and took them to a little table by a window; he weighed them, looked at them through a glass in his eye, and she stood at the counter, waiting, in cold despair. It's my last chance, she thought. Whatever he gives me is all I'll have for Nagle, and it can't possibly be enough. Maybe he'll say ten dollars. Maybe he'll cheat me. I don't know. I don't care.

He brought the things back to the counter.

"They're very nice," he said. "The settings are nice."

She was startled by his words, and his tone, mild and kind.

"Pretty old, these two," he said. "I guess you think a lot of them."

Tears came into her eyes. All she could do was to ignore them, and keep on looking at him.

"Maybe you'd rather have a smaller loan," he said, "so it'll be easier to get them back?"

She shook her head.

"No, thank you," she said, unsteadily. "As much as possible, please."

"I can let you have six hundred and twenty-five on these," he said.

"Okay!" she said, suddenly and clearly.

"Or maybe we could bring it up to six-fifty," he said, looking down at the things.

"Thank you," said Lucia. "Can I get the money today?"

"Right now," he said.

"Will you—are you going to put them into the window?" she asked, still ignoring the tears on her cheeks.

"Oh, no!" he said. "That's only the things for sale." He glanced up. "Y'see, if you don't redeem the things, or you fail to pay the interest for a certain length of time, why, we're allowed to sell them."

"I see!" she said. "It seems—sort of pathetic, doesn't it? People's funny things."

"Sometimes," he said, "it's very pathetic. But mostly, well, you're doing a service. If anyone needs money in a hurry, well, here's where they can get it. There's been cases I know of where a man would have committed suicide if he couldn't get forty-fifty dollars quick. Then somebody'll come in here that would get put out in the street if he can't pay his rent. Well, the landlord won't take his fine watch. The landlord, naturally, he don't know the value of things. Then, say the next week, this man gets a good job. Soon as he gets his pay, he's back here, redeems his watch, and all is well."

Lucia was very much touched. I like him! she thought. He's trying to make me see that it isn't horrible and comic to be a pawnbroker. He wants it to seem sort of romantic.

She wished to help him in this; she wanted to show an interest in his business.

"Do you ever get wedding rings?" she asked.

"Well, not so many," he said. "People have a lot of sentiment about them and a wedding ring hasn't got much actual value, as a rule. Although you'd be surprised how many women throw away their wedding rings."

"But why?"

"Well, they're getting a divorce, or they're mad at their husbands, or one thing or another, and they throw away their rings."

"I saw a baby's silver mug in the window."

"The father's a drunk," he said. "That's a bad case. Well, I'll get your money for you now."

He brought it to her, all in bills.

"Good luck!" he said.

The taxi driver sat in the cab, smoking a cigarette.

"Do you know where I could get any cigarettes?" Lucia asked.

"Lady," he said, "if I knew that, I'd be rich. I can let you have one."

"Thank you!" she said. "Now I'd like to go to Stern's, please, on Forty-second Street."

He gave her a cigarette; he struck a match and held it for her, and she leaned back, relaxed, savoring the cigarette with something like bliss. It's all over, she thought. I haven't got the money, and I can't get it, ever.

I wonder if this is a little the way people feel sometimes when they're going to die, she thought. When the doctor says there's no hope, and there's nothing you can do but just let go. It would be a rather good way to die, not fighting and struggling, just letting go.

She had a picture of herself at home, lying comfortably in bed, with everything over. Nothing to be done, about anything.

But the children! she thought. And Father . . . They'd have to send a cable to Tom . . . Oh, no! You never can stop fighting and struggling.

The cab turned into Forty-second Street, and looking at her watch, she saw that she was over half an hour late. Maybe Mr. Donnelly's gone, she thought. You couldn't blame him.

But he was there, standing outside the entrance, tall, outstandingly neat, in a dark blue, double-breasted suit and a gray felt hat; not smoking, not fidgeting, not glancing around; just waiting. He certainly doesn't look like a crook, she thought. He's quite distinguished looking. Quite handsome.

As she was getting out of the cab he came forward, hat in hand.

"We could keep the cab," he said. "There's a place in the Fifties I think you would like."

She settled back in the cab and as he got in beside her, he gave the driver an address.

"I haven't got the money," she said, at once. "I never can get it."

He was silent, and she turned to look at him; she found him looking at her, with his curiously clouded blue eyes.

"Be easy," he said. "Take it easy."

Chapter Thirteen

There was no reason to feel reassured by this, but she did feel so.

"This place where we are going," he said. "There's a small room in it we can have to ourselves. Unless you'd rather eat out with the other people?"

"Maybe we could talk better by ourselves," she said.

"That's what I'd thought of," he said.

It was strange, she thought, that she had no hesitation about lunching alone with him in whatever place he had chosen. She remembered things she had read in old-fashioned novels about private dining rooms, always the scene of some amorous adventure, a seduction, drugged wine, a conniving waiter. But Mr. Donnelly isn't like that, she thought.

The cab stopped before a little restaurant of rather smart appearance, with a dark blue canopy over the entrance on which was lettered Café Colorado; a doorman in uniform came forward to open the door of the taxi. Donnelly took a bill out of his wallet and passed it to the driver.

"All right," he said.

"*What?*" said the driver. "Well, thanks. Thanks a lot."

They went down a few steps, to a carpeted restaurant with lighted lamps on small tables, and at one end a bar with a mirror lined by blue fluorescent lights. The place was well filled with people; nothing at all queer about it, she thought. An elderly waiter came hurrying up to Donnelly.

"Bon jour, madame, monsieur!"

"Tell the boss I am here, will you?" said Donnelly.

"Mais oui, monsieur!" said the waiter, and hurried away.

Very promptly a man came across the room to them, stout and swarthy, with a black mustache and sorrowful eyes.

"Ah . . . !" he said. "Ze room, Marty?"

"Parfaitement," said Donnelly.

"Zis way, madame!"

They followed him through the restaurant, and he opened a door beside the bar, leading to a dark little passage. At the end of this he opened another door.

"Voilà!" he said, with an air of pride.

"C'est assez bien," said Donnelly, and went on talking in French, of which Lucia had only a schoolgirl knowledge. She gathered, though, that he was talking about the lunch, and that the other man was called Gogo.

The room itself made her want to laugh, it was so exactly like something from one of those old-fashioned books; a small room without windows, a round table right in the center, set for two, with a bowl of red roses in the middle; there was even a couch, covered with blue and gold brocade.

"Alors . . ." said Gogo, and bowed and smiled and went out, closing the door after him.

"I did not introduce him," said Donnelly. "I did not think you'd be wanting to know him."

"Well, why not? Is he—?" She paused for a word. "Is he—questionable?"

"He is a good friend of mine," Donnelly said. "Only, he's not the class you're used to."

'Class'? she thought. What 'class' would you call Donnelly? According to his own words, he came of peasant stock; he had had no education; he was a blackmailer and God knew what else. But he had a courtesy that was natural and effortless; his speech had a correctness, a rhythm like that of a carefully trained foreigner. I don't know what he is, she thought.

He drew back a chair for her.

"I ordered a Martini for you," he said. "Will that be what you like?"

"Oh, yes, thanks!"

"Will you have a cigarette?" he said. "While you're waiting?"

He lit one for her, and one for himself; he moved an ash tray nearer to her, and sat down across the table from her.

"You speak French very fluently, don't you?" she said.

"It is fluent enough," he said, "but I don't know at all if it is very good. I picked it up in Quebec."

"Did you live in Quebec?"

"I was in a monastery near there for more than a year."

"In a monastery?"

"It was in my mind, those days, that I'd study to be a priest."

"Oh! Did you change your mind?"

"I had no vocation," he said, and after a pause, "the world was too much with me."

It seemed to Lucia then that this big, stalwart man, of unimaginable experiences, was a creature infinitely more sensitive and more fragile than herself. She had thought that often about David, about her father, about Tom; she had felt herself to be tougher, more flexible, better able to endure what must come.

"Didn't you ever marry?" she asked.

"I wanted to marry," he said, "but I never found a girl would suit me."

A slight resentment rose in her, against this male arrogance.

"You never found anyone good enough?" she asked.

"I did not," he answered, with simplicity.

The waiter came in then, with one cocktail on a tray.

"Aren't you having one?" she asked.

"I never take a drink till five o'clock."

"Why not?" she asked, a little sharply.

"There was a time when I drank too much," he said. "For three years I went roaring around, till I had the d.t.'s. It is a terrible thing. You'd never forget it. To Bellevue, they took me, and I saw the others that were in it. Old men, some of them, with their lives all drunk away and wasted." He paused. "Now I am moderate," he said.

"You've had quite a lot of experience . . ." she said, lightly.

"I have that," he said.

She sipped the cocktail, feeling an odd new strength in herself, a sense of power she had not known before. I can manage *him,* all right, she thought.

"You look very charming," he said. "It is a nice little hat you're wearing, and the white gloves, and all."

Then it all came back to her.

"I don't feel charming," she said, bitterly. "I've—failed. I can't get that money."

"You were trying?"

"I went to a loan company I saw advertised," she said.

"They said they lent money on your note, without any red tape. Well, they wouldn't." She was silent for a moment, remembering Miss Poser. She opened her purse and took out the manila envelope, into which she had put the money. "Here's six hundred and fifty dollars," she said. "That's all I can get. *All.*"

"Did you draw that out of your bank?"

"No. I haven't anything in the bank except what I have to use. No. I pawned some jewelry I had."

"Give me the ticket," he said.

"But—why?"

"Give me the ticket," he said, with a ring in his voice.

"But why? I don't want to."

"Give it me!" he said, rising.

"No! I won't!"

He stood over her, his hand outstretched, and she was startled, and almost frightened, by the power of the man, the concentrated force in him. His face was not blurred now; the angle of his jaw was sharp; his eyes were clear and cold.

"Give it me! Get it out of your purse."

She took the ticket out of her purse, reluctant and angry.

"Well, why?" she demanded.

"I will get your things back for you," he said. "Every damn one of them."

"They're not important. I don't care about them."

He began walking up and down the room.

"I will get them back for you," he said.

"I don't care about them!" she cried. "I only want to stop that Nagle."

"I will do that, too," he said.

"Oh! But can you?"

"I didn't know how it was—" he began, when the waiter came in, with shrimp cocktails set in ice.

"Bring the lady another Martini," said Donnelly, and she made no protest.

He sat down at the table.

"I didn't know it would be so bad for you," he said. "Carlie—Nagle, that is, told me he'd looked into it. He said you'd plenty of money; your father, too."

"I haven't any money," she said. "Only what I have to use."

"It's a wonder they wouldn't give you some."

"They do! My father and my husband have always given me anything I wanted."

"It is not enough," he said.

"You mean I ought to have a little special fund—to pay blackmail out of?"

She could see that that hit him, hard, and she was glad.

"I don't care about those bits of jewelry," she said. "I only care about saving my daughter from a miserable scandal."

"I'm not worrying about your daughter. She would get over a scandal."

The waiter came back with the second Martini and set it before her.

"I'll have a talk with Nagle," he said. "I will try to make him wait till the money comes in from the deal we've got on. I'd pay him for you now, only the two of us are hard up, putting all we could lay hands on into this new thing. The trouble is, Nagle is always nervous if he hasn't a good sum in the bank. Drink your cocktail."

"I don't want it."

"Then eat your lunch."

"I can't."

"Look!" he said. "If I cannot keep Nagle quiet, then let him go ahead. He will take the letters to your father—"

"No! He can't! He mustn't!"

"Your father is a fine old gentleman, by what I saw. He will not be too hard on the girl."

"No! No!" she said. "My father *mustn't* know."

"You take it too hard. Let Nagle go ahead. It will soon be over—"

"No!" she cried, again. "You don't understand. Father can't know anything at all about Ted Darby."

She pushed back her chair, but she did not rise; she sat there rigid, thinking fast. If I tell Lieutenant Levy, Father'll have to know. Have to know about Bee and Ted; have to know that he killed Ted. And I can't let that Murray stay in jail. I've got to tell Lieutenant Levy, unless . . .

Unless somehow Murray could be got out of prison—without my telling the police.

"What is it?" Donnelly asked. "What is it worrying you?"

She glanced quickly at him, and the look in his face was clear to her. She did not care to put it into words for herself; simply she knew that she could trust him with anything at all. She knew that she could make use of all the strength and the force in him.

"Father would go straight to the police, if Mr. Nagle saw him," she said. "And if the police find out about my daughter and Ted Darby—"

"They would not care about that," he said. "When it is people like yourselves, they'd try to keep the girl's name out of it. Her letters have nothing to do with Darby's killing."

"But suppose they have?"

"They have not."

Her heart was beating in a quick, erratic way that made her breath come too fast.

"Suppose it wasn't Murray who killed Ted?" she said.

"I know damn well it was not Murray," he said. "Murray was framed."

"But he's in jail for it. He'll be tried for it."

"He will go to the chair for it," said Donnelly. "I would not lose a night's sleep over that. He and Darby, the two of them, were dirty, double-crossing——" He checked himself. "They are rats," he said.

"Murray can't be punished—executed—for something he didn't do."

"Don't worry about him. He is not worth it."

"Could you get Murray off, if you wanted?"

"I would not want to."

"But *could* you, if you tried? Please answer!"

"I might," he said. "Why do you want to know?"

The waiter came in, and hesitated, seeing the untouched shrimps.

"Wait a while," said Donnelly. "Is there a bell in it? There? Then take it easy till I'll ring for you."

The man went out, closing the door behind him.

"You could get Murray freed?" she asked.

"Maybe. Only I would not lift a finger to do it."

She had the most vivid image in her mind of yesterday's brunch, the blue water, the green trees, the sunny tranquillity; Mrs. Lloyd's smile, the way Owen had watched Bee. Bee, and David, and her father, and Tom so very far away, all of them so innocent, all of them threatened by these dark, horrible shadows from another world, Ted Darby, Nagle, Murray, criminals, all of them, cruel, dangerous as wild beasts.

"What is it worrying you?" Donnelly asked.

"Well . . . Suppose I told you *I* killed Ted Darby?" she said.

Chapter Fourteen

He gave her a quick side-long look.

"No," he said. "You could not kill anyone."

"It was an accident. He was—I got angry at him, about the letters. I pushed him, and he fell. It was in the boat-house, and he fell into the launch, on the anchor. It killed him."

He gave her another of those sidelong looks, wary and alert.

"Swallow your drink," he said. "It will do you good."

She shook her head.

"I didn't know he was dead, until the morning," she said. "Then I found him there. Then I took him over to the island. It was . . . It was—" She paused a moment. "I had —to get him off the anchor. It was . . . And then I had— to get him out of the boat."

Her voice was unsteady, her mouth trembled. Remembering it was worse than the doing of it.

"You'll have to believe me," she said.

She looked up at him; their eyes met for a long moment.

"I do believe you," he said. "There's no saint in heaven would do more than you'd do for your family."

"I was—never going to tell anyone," she said. "But now —I can't let Murray pay for it."

"You can that," he said. "Murray's no good at all."

"That doesn't matter. I can't let him suffer for something that's my fault."

"You can."

"No," she said. "I won't. It's a sin."

"A sin?" he repeated, as if startled. "It's hard, now, to know what's a sin and what isn't."

"It's never hard," she said. "You always know in your own heart what's right."

"Ah . . ." he said. "It's not that easy. You have to look at all sides of it. Now, there's your family. They're good people. They do good in the world. What's the sense in sacrificing them for a rat like Murray? You have to think out what's going to do the most good."

"No," she said. "You have to do what's right, no matter what comes of it."

"There are many don't agree with that," he said. "There are many believe you have to study out what's going to do the most good in the end."

"That's——" she began, and stopped herself. That's Jesuitical, she had been going to say, but maybe that was his belief. "I can't see things that way," she said. "I can't let Murray stay in jail. No matter what happens to us. I'd rather be in jail myself."

"You'll not go to jail," he said. "Look, now. Will you not try to eat a little? I've ordered a steak, but if there's something else——"

"That man's in prison this moment—while I sit here."

"Look, now. It doesn't mean to him what it would mean to you. He's been in it before."

"Oh, can't you understand how I feel?" she cried. "I can't

sit here—eating . . . I don't know what to do. I don't know where to turn."

"Turn to me," he said.

She looked at him. He pushed back his chair and rose, and began to walk up and down the room again. He was a big man, and heavy, but his heel-and-toe walk was very light; his gleaming shoes seemed more flexible than anyone else's.

"It's my punishment," he said. "I've been a fool with my money, and worse. And now, when I need it, I haven't it. I'd give the eyes out of my head if I could pay off Nagle now. Or if I'd the money to pay Isaacs or Jimmy Downey to get Murray off." At the end of the room he turned and came back toward her. "Only don't be eating your heart out," he said. "I will do it."

"How?"

"I will work on Nagle," he said. "He knows we'll be getting this money before long, and I will pay him out of the share that's coming to me."

"Why should you?" she demanded, angrily. "Why should *you* pay blackmail to that horrible man, if he's your partner, or whatever you call him?"

"Well, you see," he said, "it was Nagle got the letters from Darby. Nagle thought up the whole thing. He has a right—"

"You can't talk like that! As if it was an ordinary business thing. It's—don't you realize it's a *crime*?"

He was coming toward her, so big, light-footed, his eyes blank. He was menacing. Then he wheeled round and went away from her.

"Yes . . ." he said. "Yes, you're right. God help me, I

hardly know any more what's right from what's wrong."

"Everyone knows."

"Yes," he said. "But I cannot go back on Nagle now."

"Even when you realize that he's a criminal?"

"I am a criminal myself," he said.

"You're not," said Lucia. "Not really."

"I've broken the law," he said. "I've done wrong enough. Only, God be praised, I never killed anyone." He was down at the end of the room now, with his back to her. "Only in the war," he said, "the first war, I mean. And the killing in the war is not accounted a sin." He was silent for a time. "But I wasn't easy about it," he said. "I was young then, and when I'd see some of the Boches—that's what we called them, in those days—when I'd see them lying dead in a field or maybe a forest, I'd think, was it me did that? And now, when you see the young lads going off again . . . You'd think the devil rules the world."

He came back to her.

"There's yourself," he said. "So good—and look at the trouble that's come to you. But I'll get you free of it. I'll work on Nagle, and I will see Isaacs or Downey, about getting Murray out."

"But how can they? Unless they find someone else?"

"Isaacs can get anyone off," said Donnelly.

"But what will you tell him? Will you have to say that you know someone else did it?"

"I will tell him nothing at all. He'll go to see Murray, and they will fix it up together." He paused a moment. "Will you trust me?" he asked.

"Yes . . ." she said.

"There is nothing I would not do for you," he said. "Nothing in the world."

She lowered her eyes, not to see the look in his face.

"Could we have the steak?" she asked. "I've got to be getting home."

He rang the bell at once.

"Did you ever get a ham?" he asked.

"Oh, yes!" she said, and added, "Thank you."

"There's a roast of beef on the way," he said. "And three pounds of bacon."

"Mr. Donnelly—"

"Yes?"

"I'd rather you didn't send anything more. It's–hard to explain them. And—"

"Yes?"

"Well, they're black market, aren't they?"

"I suppose you'd call them that," he said. "But there's no need for it to be on your conscience at all. They are a present to you."

"Thank you very much, but please don't send the beef. Please don't send anything."

"I'm afraid they're on the way, if they're not there already."

The waiter brought in the steak, French fried potatoes, peas, a salad; he moved saltcellars, emptied the ash tray, and went away.

"That Sibyl is a fine woman," said Donnelly.

"But you don't know her!"

"I had a bit of a talk with her yesterday, when you were not home," he said. "She is a fine woman."

"Yes. She is."

"I asked her to let me know if ever I was needed," he said. "I gave her my telephone number."

How could you be 'needed'? Lucia thought. But she did not say it.

"Eat, will you not?" he asked, anxiously. "You're pale. Eat a bit of the red meat. And take it easy. I will get Murray out of jail for you, and I will keep Nagle off your neck. He'll give you the letters back. Trust me, will you not?"

"I do trust you," she said.

He gave a sigh, as if a weight were lifted. But he did not eat, nor could she. This room without windows was quiet, too quiet; she felt unbearably restless. She did something unusual to her; she opened her purse and took out a little mirror and looked at herself.

She did not look flustered and frightened now. It was true that she was pale, her hair a little disordered, but there was something in her face she had not seen in it before, a sorrowful and quiet beauty. That's how I look to him, she thought.

Chapter Fifteen

They did not want the dessert; he waved it away. No check was brought to him; he left some bills on the table, and they went out of the room, through the restaurant, and into the street. He stopped a taxi and took her to the train.

"You'll be hearing from me," he said. "And you'll take it easy, will you not? I'll look after everything."

She stood silent, her lashes lowered. She knew that he was looking at her; she knew that she was dark, slender and lovely; she knew he was waiting for her to look up, and presently she raised her eyes.

"Thank you," she said.

"Could I come to the house?" he asked. "Just once more? Stop by, maybe, and bring a bottle of Scotch for your father?"

"I'm sorry," she said, "I'm very sorry, but—not possibly."

"Can I see you once more?" he said. "When I've settled all this, would you have lunch with me, the way it was today?"

She did not answer.

"Just the once, when it's all settled?" he asked. "I know how it is with you. You have your family and your—social position to think of. But if you'd give me just one more sight of you . . . ?"

There were people moving and hurrying all around them; a prodigious voice was announcing trains. But they were somehow isolated. He did not urge her any more; he simply waited, in a dreadful humility. The gate of her platform was opening, but still she stood there, with her lashes lowered.

Suddenly she held out her white-gloved hand, and looked at him.

"Yes," she said. "I'll be very pleased to have lunch with you someday."

She did not smile; they never smiled at each other. He held her hand for a moment, very lightly.

"Be easy," he said.

She went along the dim platform, in a silent, smooth-moving crowd; she got into a car. It was a smoker, and she decided to stay in it and have a cigarette. She sat down beside a man and opened her purse; she took out her pack, but it was empty; she felt in the corners; she turned it upside down.

"Have one of mine!" said the man beside her.

"Oh, but really . . . ! When they're so hard to get . . ."

"Not hard for *me,*" he said. "Take one! Take one!"

He lit it for her; a burly man with a red face and bright little blue eyes.

"This shortage'll be over in a week or so," he said. "But in the meantime it doesn't bother *me* any. I've got connections in just about every line of business *you* ever heard of. Why, only the other day, this fellow I know was squawking about an alarm clock. Couldn't find one anywhere. I'll get you one this afternoon, I told him. Hey, no black market stuff for me, he says. I don't use the black market, brother, I tell him. I use *this.*"

He tapped his temple with his third finger and raised his thin brows; he smiled, with his lips closed. And he was trying to impress her. His little bright eyes flickered over her, not boldly, but with admiration.

"Here!" he said. "Let's change seats. You young ladies always like to sit by the window."

When he stood up, he put his hand into his pocket, and brought out two packs of cigarettes, Mr. Harper's favorite brand.

"Just slip these in your purse," he said.

"Oh, I couldn't!"

"Plenty more where they came from," he said. "You take them. You'll be doing me a favor."

He settled down cozily beside her.

"No, sir," he said, "I never married. I see you're wearing the badge of servitude." He laughed. "That's the way it goes," he said. "Every time I meet an attractive young lady, she's got a husband. Didn't bother to wait for me."

Now he got around to asking questions, and she had no objection to telling him that she had a husband overseas, that she had two children. Just like somebody in a magazine story, she thought.

"It's hard," he said, gravely, "it's very hard. Attractive young lady."

He's a wolf, she thought. But not a bad one. Sort of pathetic. She could see what he was getting around to now.

"I could meet you somewhere . . ." he said. "We could have a little dinner, go somewhere to dance. Do you good."

"I can't leave the children," she said. "I never go out in the evenings."

"Mistake," he said. "Great mistake. You could get one of these high-school kids to sit with the children."

He obviously pictured two small children, and let him, Lucia thought. She was surprised at herself for the bland enjoyment she found in his company. But she would not tell him her name.

"No," she said, looking into his eyes. "Really I can't."

"I'll give you my card," he said, "and if ever you change your mind—"

Mr. Richard Hoopendyke. Representing the Shilley Mfg. Co.

"Change your mind!" he said, rising when she did.

"Well, maybe . . ." said Lucia.

When she got out at the familiar station, it was strange to see the sunny afternoon quiet. It seemed to her that she had been gone so long, so very long; she felt timid about going home, as if she had in some way changed. She got into a taxi with two other people, a man and a woman, and they rode in grim silence. They don't like me, Lucia told herself. They think I'm queer. An Undesirable Acquaintance. Well, maybe I am.

She felt queer. She was the first one to get out, and she told the driver to stop at the corner; she walked down the road, feeling strangely solitary. Such a long day, she thought, and so much has happened.

But, after all, what really had happened? She had tried to get a loan, and failed; she had pawned her jewelry. And then I had lunch . . . she thought. There's nothing so wonderful in all that. Only, I never can tell anyone about it. Certainly not Father and the children, and not even Tom. Tom would know there wasn't anything wrong, but he wouldn't like it. Lunch in a private room. With a crook. Tom wouldn't like that man in the smoker, and neither would Father or the children. They don't think I'm like that.

The house seemed unwelcoming in the late afternoon sun. It's nice when someone comes out to meet you, she thought. When the children were little, they always rushed out. That was nice. But then I always had some little present for them.

And she was empty-handed now; she felt it. She was bringing back nothing. The front door was unlocked, as usual; she opened it and went in, and Mr. Harper spoke, from the sitting room.

"Lucia?"

"It's me, Father."

He was sitting in an armchair, with a book in his hand, an empty teacup on the table beside him.

"Oh . . . Sibyl gave you your tea?" she said.

"Never forgets," he said.

She came up behind him, and kissed his silver head.

"Ha . . ." he said, pleased. "Have a good day, m'dear?"

"Yes, thank you, Father."

"Shopping, I suppose," he said. "Your mother used to come home, say she was exhausted, shopping all day. I'd ask her what she'd bought, and half the time she'd say she hadn't bought anything at all."

He laughed, his eyes fixed upon nothing; as if in his mind he could see that absurd and beloved figure. Lucia handed him one of the packs of cigarettes Mr. Hoopendyke had given her.

"That's very nice," he said. "Very welcome, m'dear. By the way, that Lloyd boy was here. Wanted my permission to put my name up at the Yacht Club. I told him my sailing days were a thing of the past. I shouldn't make much use of the club. But I didn't like to rebuff the boy. Nice lad. And the dues are no great matter. I told him to go ahead, if he liked."

He wants to belong to the club, Lucia thought. He's lonely. I don't keep him from being lonely. I haven't any time. I don't know what I do with myself, but I never have any time.

"You'll be on a committee inside a week," she said. "You always are."

"Nonsense!" he said. "At my age—"

"Nonsense yourself!" she said. "People always have such confidence in you, Daddy."

" 'Daddy' . . ." he repeated. She had not used that name for a long time, and it seemed to echo for both of them. Tears came into her eyes and she winked them away.

"I've got to see Sibyl," she said.

Sibyl was standing at the cabinet, in a dazzle of sun, breaking eggs, letting the whites slip into one fluted blue bowl, and the golden yolks into a green one. It was a delicate operation, and beautiful. She dealt with the egg in hand, and then looked up, with her tender, slow smile.

"Oh, you're back, ma'am?"

"Yes, I'm back. We're having the cold ham tonight, aren't we, Sibyl?"

"Thought I'd better cook the beef tonight, ma'am."

"The beef . . . ?"

"It came just in time," said Sibyl. "And I'll make the Yorkshire pudding Mr. Harper likes."

No questions about that beef. No questions, ever, about anything. But what does she *think?* Lucia asked herself.

Above everything in the world, she wanted to know what Sibyl thought.

"It was a present," she said.

"Yes, ma'am," said Sibyl.

"You must have been surprised, when the beef came," Lucia said.

"No, ma'am."

"Well, why not?"

"Mr. Donnelly told me he was sending it, ma'am. Asked me, what would Mrs. Holley like. Said he'd get anything you wanted, any time."

The words, in Sibyl's soft voice, had an impact that made Lucia catch her breath. Nobody should say that. Nobody should know that.

"I've told him not to send anything more," she said. "I've told him not to come here again."

"Yes, ma'am," said Sibyl.

Now drop it! Lucia told herself. Let well enough alone. But she could not.

"He's not the sort of person to have here," she said.

"He's unfortunate," said Sibyl.

"What do you mean, Sibyl?"

"Got in bad company," said Sibyl.

"He's a free agent. He could choose his company, like anyone else."

"We don't always know what we're doing, ma'am," said Sibyl. "Till it's too late."

"It's never too late to—change," said Lucia.

"That's what my husband says, all the time. But I don't think people change much."

"I didn't know you'd been married, Sibyl."

"Yes, ma'am. He's in jail, in Georgia."

"Oh, Sibyl!"

"Been there eighteen years," Sibyl said, "and got seven more to go. Unless he gets a parole. And he won't."

"And you're—waiting for him?" Lucia asked.

"Obliged to," Sibyl answered, somberly. "Bill never did me any wrong. Not that he knew of. When they took him away, I told him I'd wait for him, and I have."

"Eighteen years!" Lucia said. "That must have been terribly hard for you, Sibyl."

"Yes, ma'am," said Sibyl. "And I don't know if it was sensible, either."

"You mean you've changed your mind about him, Sibyl?"

"It just didn't do him much good," Sibyl said. "He's got a hopeful nature. Thinks he can come out of jail, when he's fifty-four years old, and start a fine new life for us. Gets more and more philosophical."

"Well . . ." Lucia said, anxiously. "That's probably a good thing, Sibyl."

"Maybe so, ma'am," said Sibyl, with courteous deference. "The philosophy Bill's got, it's that everything that happens is for the best. He doesn't study about injustice. He's not bitter, shut up there all the best years of his life for what wasn't wrong at all."

"What was it, Sibyl?"

"Bill was a sailor," said Sibyl. "I reckon that's why I married him; I was just so crazy to travel. Don't know how it got in my head, but even when I was a little girl, I used to think about it. Maybe it was out of books. The white people my mother worked for used to lend me books. I used to think, if I could ever get up to the frozen North, big, white fields of snow, those lights in the sky . . . And Paris. Bill told me it's all true about Paris. Colored people can go anywhere, see all the sights. Bill said we'd get to take trips."

"Didn't you ever?"

"No, ma'am. First thing we got married, I started to have a baby. And he gave up going to sea. He got a job in the mill; said he wanted to be near me, case there was any trouble. I lost the baby, and there he was. We had some money saved, and he said we'd take a trip. Went to a steamship office to buy us a ticket. Man said they didn't want any niggers on their ships. Bill said it was the law that he could buy a ticket if he had the money. The man hit him, and Bill hit him back. Assault with intent to kill, they called it. But the man didn't die, and Bill didn't ever think to kill him. He just hit back. He had a knife on him, but he always did, ever since the days when he was at sea."

"Maybe when he gets out, you can take a trip."

"No, ma'am," said Sibyl. "Bill'll be fifty-four, and I don't know if he can get him a decent job. He's got kind of queer, shut up in that jail. I reckon I'll have to support him. Well, I can do it, if I keep my health."

"Well . . ." Lucia said. "You must have been a wonderful help and comfort to your husband, all this while."

"I don't know . . ." said Sibyl. "He's got that philosophical nature . . . If I'd said I wouldn't be waiting for him, he'd have found some other kind of comfort. And I'd have found some way to see the world."

Lucia was silent, deeply impressed by this glimpse into Sibyl's nature. All these years, while she had gone about her work so quietly and competently, there had been in her this passionate longing to see the world. I never had that, Lucia thought. I never specially thought about traveling. I never wanted anything like that. *What did I want?*

She had wanted a husband and children, and she had got them. Ever since she could remember, everything she had wanted had been given to her. If she had wanted a doll, a bicycle, a new dress, her parents had given it to her. The husband she wanted had appeared while she was still in school; the son and the daughter she wanted had come to her without too much pain and effort.

Was she, then, a creature uniquely favored? Or was she a creature, not favored, but scorned and dismissed by life, denied what other people had? There was David, filled with his uneasy hopes, Bee and her stormy follies, Tom going through the experience he could never share with her. Even Sibyl. Even Donnelly . . .

I'm like a doll, she thought. I'm not real. As she sat at dinner with her family, this sense of unreality became almost frightening. They told about things that had happened to them today, and it was all real, and crystal-clear, to be understood by anyone. But her day was like a dream; if she should try to describe it, who would believe or understand about the vaults, the loan office, the pawnshop, the private dining room, even Mr. Hoopendyke in the smoker?

She sat down to write to Tom, with the same sense of numbed unreality. Who was this, trying to write a letter?

DEAR TOM:

I don't know where you are. I don't know who I am. Tom, I'm in such trouble . . .

Take it easy, Donnelly had said. I'll get Murray out, he had said. I'll keep Nagle quiet. But she could not take it easy. She was caught in a current that was carrying her farther and farther from the shore.

Her restless dreams that night were all of the sea. She

dreamed that she was swimming, in a race with Mrs. Lloyd, and everyone she loved best was standing on the shore, watching. Mrs. Lloyd, in a little hat of purple violets, went through the water with incredible speed and ease, and Lucia went laboring after her, disappointing her own people so by her clumsy floundering.

She waked from that, and got up in haste, to look at the letter she had written to Tom, to make sure that she had not really written anything about 'trouble,' or even anything he might read between the lines. I don't think so . . . she said to herself. It seems to me just like my other letters. Just babbling.

She went back to bed, and she dreamed that she was in a rowboat, with an enormous rock on the thwarts. She pulled on the oars with all her strength, but she could not move the boat with that great weight in it. And she had to move; she had to hurry. At first it was because something was coming after her, out of the dark boathouse, something dangerous and dreadful. But, as she strained at the oars, she became aware that the danger was the rock itself. If she did not hurry, did not get to the place of safety, the rock was going to change into something else.

It was beginning already. Two things like ears were shaping on its top; it shifted a little, and she thought it sighed. Then it rolled toward her, and she waked, in a sweat of terror. There was a great wind blowing, and rain was driving in at the open window; there was a noise, as if the night itself were roaring.

She sprang up and closed her window and barefoot, in her pajamas, went out into the hall, to Bee's room. It was dark in there, and filled with the rushing wind, and her daughter lay there, unconscious, helpless. She closed that window, and went to David's room. He too was asleep, and the rain was driving straight on his back. She pulled off the damp sheet and covered him with a blanket, and he did not stir.

Tears were running down her face, it so pierced her heart to think of her children lying unprotected in the rain. She went along the hall to her father's room, and there was a light showing under the door; she knocked and he said "Come in! Come in!" in his steady old voice.

He was standing by the window in his flannel dressing gown, smoking a cigarette.

" 'Oh, pilot, 'tis a fearful night,' what, what?" he said.

"Yes, it *is!*" said Lucia.

"What's this? What's this? Are you crying, m'dear?"

"It's just the rain. I was closing the children's windows."

"Sit down and have a cigarette," he said. "I've got that pack you brought me, m'dear. Here! Sit down here. Very comfortable chair."

Chapter Sixteen

"I wish you'd ask Mrs. Lloyd to tea," Bee said at breakfast, with a hint of reproach.

"Well, I will," said Lucia. "I'll call her up after breakfast."

"There's the postman!" cried David, jumping up.

He went to the door, and came back leisurely, looking through the sheaf of letters he carried.

"Oh, hurry up!" said Bee. "Is there anything for me?"

"Take it easy!" said David.

"Mother, tell him to hurry up!" said Bee.

"*Take* it easy! *Take* it easy!" said David. "Four for you, Mother; two V-mails from Dad. One for you, Grandpa. Letter for me from Dad. And here's the vitally important mail for Miss Beatrice Holley. Letter from your alumnae association, letter from Boothbay—that must be Edna. Oh, gosh! Here's a letter from Jerry, Bee. Open it and let's see if he's still in China."

"When I'm good and ready," said Bee.

They all sat at the table, opening their letters. The V-mails from Tom looked queer, Lucia thought; his sharp, clear writing was unfamiliar in this diminished form. These were not the actual letters he had written; this was not the paper his hand had touched; these dwarf letters had been handled and read by heaven knew how many people.

Have written to David sending some snaps. I'd be very glad to get pictures of the house. Glad to think of you all there, out of the city. Don't worry about your letters being 'dull,' old girl. They're just what I want. They give me the feeling of our life going on, the same old way. I lived in heaven, but I didn't know it. End of paper. Love to you, kids, Granddad. Most to you.

In the second letter he wrote:

Like to hear all the little details. Other men tell me their wives complain of shortages, meat, butter, and so on. How are you getting on? You never say anything much, old girl.

Tom . . . she kept saying to herself. Tom . . . And she thought that if he were to walk into the room this moment, she would have nothing else to say to him. Only his name; only Tom.

"Will you call up Mrs. Lloyd now, Mother?" Bee asked. "If you don't, you'll forget all about it."

"I don't forget everything," said Lucia.

"Oh, Mother!" Bee protested, laughing.

"I don't find your mother forgetful," said Mr. Harper. "On the contrary. Remembers everything, it seems to me. You must realize, young lady, that a woman with a family and a house to look after has a great deal on her mind. Like an executive in an office."

"Yes, I know, Grandpa. I was only teasing her."

"Well . . ." said Mr. Harper, somewhat mollified. "You'll understand, one of these days, Beatrice, when you have a home of your own."

"Excuse me?" said David. "I promised to meet a kid."

"Wait a minute!" Bee said, and ran after him; Lucia could see them talking in the hall.

Their friendship pleased her beyond measure, but it was always a little surprising. She remembered a day, long ago, when they had been little more than babies, perhaps three and five. She had been writing a letter in the sitting room, and they had been in their nursery, with the door open. And, while she sought something to put into the letter, she had heard them talking. Those two baby creatures, that she had brought into the world, were living a life of their own, independent of her. They could talk to each other.

She had listened to them with rapture; it was a thing so thrilling that even now she remembered their talk. They had been making a baby plan. "You get your horse, David," Bee had said, "and I'll get Lilacker." That was her favorite, sacred doll, kept in a drawer; before this, she had always played alone with Lilacker; only now was the little brother admitted. Why, even if I died, they'd go on! Lucia had thought, delighted.

Why do you talk so damn much about "if you died"? Tom had asked her once. I can't say I enjoy it. Well . . . she had said. I don't exactly know. Maybe having children makes you feel like that. It doesn't make me feel like that, Tom had said. I've got insurance for you all; I've made the best arrangements I can. But I don't keep thinking about dying, all the time.

It's probably morbid, Lucia thought. It's probably some sort of enormous conceit. But it doesn't go away. When they were little, I used to feel that nobody else could understand how Bee felt about Lilacker. I used to think that nobody else would understand why David wouldn't say his prayers right. He just couldn't say "I pray the Lord my soul to take." He always said "keep." He didn't want anyone to "take" his soul. It frightened him. I'm still like that. I still think I'm the only one . . .

She telephoned to Mrs. Lloyd.

"I'd love to come!" said Mrs. Lloyd. "This afternoon? But I'm afraid Phyllis can't come; she has a dancing lesson. Would half-past four be too early? Because if I'm not home at *least* an hour before dinner, everything gets so queer. *Why* is it that just when dinner is served everyone locks itself up in a bathroom? They read; I know that. Or if they don't do that, they start making simply endless telephone calls. It must be psychological—but why *should* everyone be so psychological about not wanting dinner the moment it's put on the table?"

Mrs. Lloyd soothed Lucia; she liked her.

"Mrs. Lloyd is coming to tea," she told Sibyl. "Could you make some of those tiny biscuits, Sibyl?"

"Make popovers, ma'am," said Sibyl. "They don't take any shortening. Or we could have nice little ham sandwiches."

"Well, no," said Lucia.

She could not offer any of that ham to Mrs. Lloyd; it would be improper, even treacherous.

"Now, about the marketing?" she said. "I'll go this morning."

"Not much to get today," said Sibyl, with an air of satisfaction. "Got plenty of meat in the house. And now we can use more red points for butter."

She read off the list she had written.

"And if you'd stop in the gas company office, ma'am," she said, "maybe you could make them send a man about the icebox."

"I'll try," said Lucia.

She was surprised when Bee volunteered to go with her.

"I've got some things to get in the drugstore," Bee said. "Let's take the car."

"No," said Lucia. "I'd rather save the gas for sometime when we really need it."

They were both ready and waiting when the taxi came; Lucia in an old red and white checked gingham dress, stiffly starched, Bee in gray slacks and a white shirt, and that look she sometimes had of severely perfect grooming, her blonde hair pinned up under a blue bandanna, her arched, delicate brows a little darkened. She looked older this way; only when she turned away her head Lucia noted the sweet contour of her cheek, her childish neck.

"You're going to be disappointed, Mother," she said, "but I don't want to study art any more."

"I shan't be disappointed, dear."

"I'll tell you what I want to do, Mother. I want to go to Miss Kearney's, for her two-year secretarial course."

"Everyone says it's a very good school."

"It's the best," said Bee. "If you graduate from Kearney you're practically certain to get a job, no matter how bad conditions are."

"Well, I think that's a good idea, darling."

"Daddy won't think so," said Bee. "He'll kick like a steer."

"I'm sure he won't," said Lucia.

"Mother, honestly . . . ! You know how Father talks about career women. He's always saying that they miss out on all the best things in life."

"Well, you probably wouldn't want to be a career woman, dear."

"Yes, I do," said Bee. "I intend to keep on working after I get married."

"But if you have children——"

"I'd get a good nurse for them, and they'd be a damn sight better off than if I was home with them all the time."

"Don't swear, dear," said Lucia. "I don't see why they'd be better off. I don't see why a mother couldn't be as good as a nurse."

"Because the sort of mother who simply stays home and has no outside life can't help being narrow-minded," said Bee.

"Well, most nurses aren't so wonderfully broad-minded, that I can see," said Lucia.

"What's more, I think every woman ought to be able to support her children," said Bee. "Nobody knows what kind of world it's going to be, after this war. If you're going to take a chance and bring children into the world, you ought to be able to look after them, no matter what happens."

"Oh, yes . . ." said Lucia.

Anything rather than be like me, she thought. I'm simply a horrible example.

They rode in silence for a time.

"This new shampoo I'm going to get says it's specially good for dry hair," said Bee. "My hair's getting frightfully dry."

"You wash it too often," said Lucia.

This was a very familiar topic.

"I read an article about some women somewhere who wash their hair every single day," said Bee. "And they're famous for their beautiful hair."

"I never wash mine more than once a week," said Lucia, "and sometimes I let it go longer than that. And you'll have to admit that it's in pretty good condition."

"That's different," said Bee.

As if I were too old to *have* any hair, Lucia thought.

"I don't see why it's different," she said, coldly. "As a matter of fact, I've got rather remarkable hair. Hairdressers always speak of it. It's very thick, and it's very healthy."

Bee glanced at her.

"I know it is, Mother," she said, gently. "David and I always say so."

She kept on looking and looking at her mother.

"Don't stare so, Bee!" cried Lucia.

"Sorry, Mother," said Bee, and turned away her gaze.

They got out of the taxi at the market.

"I'll whip over to the drugstore, and come back for you," Bee said. "Will you be long, Mother?"

"Oh, hours, probably," said Lucia.

It was not, in theory, a self-service market, but it was understaffed, and the customers had been trained to go about and find their own things, to weigh the fruit and vegetables. Then you tried to get a place at the counter, to spread out the unwieldy hoard, and if you were not alert, people pushed in ahead of you and cut you off from your supplies; they planked down their things, and sometimes knocked yours off the counter. I hate this! Lucia thought. I wish I was immensely rich and arrogant, so that people *had* to be polite to me, no matter how they felt.

"No paper towels," said the clerk. "Try on Tuesday. No sugar today. Only cheese we got is pimento, and you're lucky to get that."

The telephone rang and he went away to answer it; Lucia was still waiting his return when Bee came for her.

The girl in the gas company's office was distrait and superior.

"Oh, hasn't the man been yet?" she said. "I'll check on it, to see if he came."

"He *didn't* come," said Lucia.

"Maybe you were out," said the girl.

"We're never all out."

"Well, maybe he's been busy with emergency calls," said the girl.

"Ours is an emergency," said Lucia.

"No," said the girl, flatly. "We don't call yours an emergency. I'll check on it."

"Will you let me know when to expect the man?"

"We don't do that," said the girl. "He takes the calls in turn."

The taxi driver was an unfamiliar one, and odious.

"They ought to leave us make a charge for them big grocery bags," he said. "If trucks get paid for bundles, why not us? But no. People fill up the cab with them heavy bundles that are hard on the springs and all, and when they get out, it's a ten-cent tip."

"Give him ten cents!" Bee whispered.

"No! I might have to take him again," Lucia whispered back.

He stopped the cab before the house and Lucia leaned forward to pay the fare and give him a quarter tip. He said nothing.

"I can't get the door open!" said Bee.

"Pull the handle *down!*" said he. "Pull it hard."

"I suppose it would kill you to open the door," said Bee.

"No," he said, "and it wouldn't kill you, neither."

"Hush!" whispered Lucia.

Bee got the door open and they descended, and carried the big bags into the kitchen.

"Master David said could we have lunch a little early?" said Sibyl. "He wants to go out."

"Why, yes," said Lucia. "Half-past twelve, Bee?"

"All right," said Bee, moving away.

Lucia was about to follow her, but Sibyl came to her side.

"Mr. Nagle's here, ma'am," she said, very low.

Lucia looked at her.

"Ma'am . . . !" said Sibyl. "Sit down! There! Drink some cold water, ma'am."

"Where is he, Sibyl?"

"Put him upstairs in the boathouse, ma'am. Nobody else saw him. Told him he might have to wait quite a while, till you got a chance to see him."

Lucia sipped the water, fighting against a dreadful weakness that weighed upon her. I can't, she told herself. I can't talk to him. I can't see him. I can't—I really can't do anything. If I don't go, he'll go away.

He would not go away. She was certain of that. If she did not go to him, he would come here, to the house. I'll have to see him, she thought. I'll have to.

A furious anger sprang up in her. What's Mr. Donnelly doing? she cried to herself. What does he *mean* by saying not to worry, that *he'll* look after things?

What the *hell's* the matter with him? she thought.

Chapter Seventeen

This anger helped her.

"I'll go and see him now," she said, rising.

The swing door opened and David came into the kitchen.

"Say, look, Mother!" he said. "Just glance over this, will you?"

"What is it, dear?"

"Take a look!" he said, holding out a sheaf of papers.

"But what is it, David?" she asked. "Won't after lunch do?"

"All right," he said. "Don't bother. I've got to post it right after lunch."

He was hurt.

"Oh, then I want to see it now!" said Lucia. "Give it to me, David!"

He hesitated, but only for a moment; he held out the papers again, neatly typed pages stapled together.

Ubu stood at the mouth of the cave and turned his shaggy head from side to side. Over his shoulders was thrown a rough garment of wolf-skin and in his hand he held a stone club weighing around fifteen pounds. The cave was on a mountain-side and below him stretched the jungle, where roamed the saber-toothed tiger and other wild beasts who were the enemies of him and his.

"Is it a story, David?" she asked, glancing up.

"Sort of a good start, isn't it?" he asked. "I mean, you get interested in Ubu, don't you?"

"Oh, yes, you *do!*"

"I'll tell you what it's for," he said. "You know that Vigorex Gum program on the radio? Well, they're having a contest. Anyone under sixteen can send in a story, up to a thousand words, about any of the great inventions that changed the life of mankind. The first prize is a thousand-dollar War Bond. I bet you practically everybody will do stories about the printing press, telephone, things like that. Well, I've done the wheel. You'll see how I've worked it out."

"David, how interesting!" Lucia said. "Let's go into the sitting room while I finish it."

Nagle can just wait, she thought. Even if I was mean enough not to read David's story, I couldn't get out to the boathouse now. David would want to come with me—and what could I say?

Mr. Harper was in the sitting room, reading.

"When you've finished it, Mother," David said, "maybe Grandpa'd like to glance at it."

"Certainly! Certainly! What is it? A letter?"

"Well, it's a sort of story, in a way," David answered, laughing a little. "Don't worry, Grandpa. I'm not trying to be an author, or anything like that. I just thought I'd have a try for this prize."

Lucia sat down to read the story.

"Gosh, you're a slow reader!" said David.

"I know," said Lucia.

She was trying to make her distracted mind understand the words she read.

Ikko came out of the cave, bearing in her arms the infant just born, wrapped lovingly in the skin of a giant hare.

"Ikko! Look! Stone!" cried Ubu.

As Ubu stood watching the almost perfectly round Wonderstone rolling down the mountainside, into his brain was born the great principle of the Wheel. He saw how round stones like this could be used to transport the bodies of slain beasts . . .

"Lunch is served, ma'am," said Sibyl.

"Just a moment," said Lucia, and finished the last page. "It's *awfully* good, David."

"The thing is, is it interesting?" he asked.

"It's awfully interesting!"

"The deadline's the day after tomorrow," said David. "I didn't mean to be so late with it, but I couldn't get it right. I've got to mail it right after lunch, but I'd like Grandpa to take a look."

"I'll read it at the table, if your mother doesn't object," said Mr. Harper.

Bee came into the dining room, with a towel pinned over her hair like a Red Cross nurse.

"I tried that shampoo—" she began.

"Hush, dear!" said Lucia. "David's written a story—"

"I've read it," said Bee. "I must say I think it's pretty darn good."

"Remarkably good," said Mr. Harper. "Yes . . . The thing is, my boy, have you got all your facts straight? I mean to say, these prehistoric animals—they all existed in the same era?"

"Yes, sir," said David. "I looked them up in the library. I did quite a lot of research for this thing."

I think I have a fever, Lucia said to herself. I feel so hot.

I feel so—queer. I've got to see Nagle. Suppose he gets tired of waiting? Suppose he comes here?

As soon as he had finished lunch, David left the house, and Bee went out on the veranda, to dry her hair in the sun. I'll have to go by the back way, Lucia thought, and went into the kitchen. Through the window there she saw her father pacing leisurely up and down the lawn, hands clasped behind his back. I can't go that way, either, she thought. He'd ask me where I was going.

I must make up an excuse. I've got to get to the boathouse.

"Took some lunch out to Mr. Nagle, ma'am," said Sibyl. "Took him some of Mr. Harper's whisky."

"Oh, Sibyl, what a good idea! Was he—how was he?"

"He's quiet now, ma'am," said Sibyl.

As if he were a dangerous animal, quiet only for this moment.

"If you'll go up and lie down, ma'am," said Sibyl, "I'll tell you, soon as Mr. Harper stops his walking."

Lucia went up to her room, but she could not lie down, or even sit down. She stood by the window where she could see the boathouse.

Donnelly . . . she thought. He told me not to worry. What the hell's the matter with him? Damn him. He let this happen. He's no good. He's nothing but a crook, a liar. I hate him. Damn him.

She glanced at her watch, and panic swept over. Half-past one! It isn't good for Father to walk so long, at his age . . .

But that was his habit. On a stormy day, he would walk up and down a room for an hour or more. Oh, don't let him do that today! Or make Bee come in. I've got to get out.

She kept her eyes upon her watch now. That's a mistake, she told herself. I ought to read—or mend something. This way makes the time seem twice as long. Twenty to two . . . He *can't* walk this long.

It was a quarter to two when Sibyl knocked at the door.

"Mr. Harper's come in, ma'am," she said.

Lucia went past her and ran down the stairs, through the kitchen and out by the back door. Her father or Bee might be looking out of a window; they must not see her running. I don't want to run, anyhow, she thought. Nagle can just wait, damn him.

She walked across the grass to the boathouse and up on to the little porch; she opened the door and entered into the moldy dimness. There was no one in the room; there was not a sound to be heard. She closed the door and stood holding the knob.

"Mr. Nagle?" she called.

There was no answer. Is he—hiding? she thought. No. He's upstairs. Just sitting up there? If I go upstairs, suppose he's standing behind the door?

Suppose he tries to kill me? she thought.

That seemed to her quite possible. Nagle was mysterious to her as a creature from another planet; she did not think of him as a man, a human being; only as something wholly evil and dangerous. He's come for money, of course, she thought, and if he doesn't get any, maybe he'll try to kill me.

But suppose he wasn't there at all? Suppose he had got tired of waiting and had gone away?

Too good to be true, she told herself.

"Mr. Nagle?" she called again.

"Come up!" he called back.

The only thing to do was, to go quickly, without thinking. He was sitting in a wicker chair, in the upstairs sitting room, in shirt sleeves and lavender suspenders, his soft hat on the back of his head. The lunch tray was on the floor, and on the table beside him was a bottle of whisky and a glass.

"You took your time, all right," he said.

"I couldn't help it," said Lucia.

"All right," he said. "I've done all the waiting I'm going to do. It's ten thousand now—and I mean now."

"I can't get it."

"You can get it, off your father. I checked on him."

"No. I couldn't."

"You get it—or else."

"Or else what?"

"I take one of your girl's letters to this guy I know on a newspaper."

"Go ahead," said Lucia. "No newspaper would ever publish a letter like that."

"Wait a minute, duchess," he said. "Wait a minute. Who's talking about printing any letters? All I want is, to get this guy after you. Just let me tip him off there's a good-looking blonde mixed up in the Darby case, and he'll do the rest."

"What good do you think that's going to do you?" Lucia asked.

"Plenty, duchess. Plenty."

He wants to do me harm, she thought. He wants that, much more than he wants the money. He hates me.

And that, somehow, took away all her fear of him. He wouldn't dream of killing me, she thought, scornfully, looking at him as he sat there with his hat on the back of his head, drinking her father's whisky. I'd like to hit him, she thought. I'd like to hurt him.

"Well?" he asked. "What about it, duchess?"

"Nothing," she said. "I can't give you ten thousand dollars. Or even one thousand."

"All right," he said. "Then you and that blonde girl of yours get the first train out of here, and stay out of here."

"What a crazy idea!" said Lucia.

"Get the hell out of this town and stay out of it. Or you'll wish you was never born."

He's just bluffing, Lucia thought, surprised, and still more scornful. Just trying to frighten me. He can't really do anything.

"You needn't wait," she said. "You won't get anything."

"I'll go when I'm ready," he said. "Just now, I'm not ready."

"Suppose I call the police?"

"Go ahead! Go right ahead and call the police, duchess. I'm a friend of Ted Darby's. I know he was mixed up with that blonde girl of yours, and I'm here to see can I find out anything. So I give the cops one of her letters. And they'll make her talk."

Well, that could very well happen, if I called the police, Lucia thought. It's funny, when you think of it, but I really don't want the police getting into this, any more than he does.

"Well, duchess?" he cried.

"Stop calling me that!" she said, sharply.

"So you don't like it? That's just too bad, duchess. That's one mistake I never made, to get myself mixed up with one of you goddam society bitches."

" 'Society'?" Lucia cried. "If you think I'm a 'society woman,' you're a fool."

"Oh, no," he said. "I'm no fool. I know your kind, all right. I seen friends of mine fall for them. You're just no goddam good, any of you. Any man that gets mixed up with one of you is finished. Look at Darby and—"

"Stop it!" Lucia said. "Get out of here!"

"When I'm ready, duchess. When I'm ready."

"You—" she began, and stopped, with a chill of terror at the sound of a step on the stairs.

Father? she thought. No, no! Oh, don't let it be Father!

It was Donnelly, tall and elegant, in a slate-gray suit, with a blue cornflower in his buttonhole.

"What's this?" he asked. "I could hear the two of you from outside."

"He's going to give the letters to a newspaperman—" said Lucia.

"Shut up!" said Nagle.

"Let her alone," said Donnelly. "What are you doing here at all, Carlie? It is a dirty, underhanded thing for you to do, when we had it all fixed up."

He spoke with severity, but not angrily.

"You got your money," he said. "Why wouldn't that be enough for you, Carlie? You'd no right to come here."

"Now you look here, Marty," said Nagle, rising. "If we got to have a showdown, we got to have a showdown. I come here, because some way I got to get this woman off your neck. You don't see it, but I do. She's going to ruin you."

"Let her alone," said Donnelly, still without anger. "It is a thing beyond your understanding, entirely."

"The hell it is!" said Nagle. "Look what she done to you already. A man like you, a man with a name—and yesterday you were passing the hat, getting a couple of hundred here, couple of hundred there. D'you think I want the money you got that way? Listen. We went in this together; we were cutting fifty-fifty. And when she won't come across, what do you do? Pass the hat—to pay *me*. Like I was holding you up. I am not. I don't want your money."

"Well, you took it," said Donnelly, "and you told me you'd let her alone. You are a liar, Carlie."

"So I'm a liar. Okay. I'm not going to let her alone."

"You will have to," Donnelly said.

Lucia moved aside, so that she could lean against the wall. The two men stood facing each other; Nagle was shorter, he was overweight, he looked older, but there was a powerful energy about him, in the pugnacious set of his head, in the way he stood, with his rear thrust out. And Donnelly was blurred, vague; he showed no energy, only that severe patience.

But he'll settle things, she thought. One way or another. She leaned against the wall, completely passive. There was nothing for her to do, or to say; for the moment there was nothing she need think about. The two men were talking, but she did not listen to them. She was waiting; she was resting.

Until a note in Donnelly's voice startled her. She glanced at him, and his blurred look was gone; he was wary, his head a little bent, like a listening animal.

"What did yez say?" he asked.

"You heard me," said Nagle.

They're afraid of each other, Lucia thought, seeing in Nagle the same alertness, the same bodily stillness. As if the least little movement might make the other pounce.

"You told me Eddy and Moe were talking about it," said Donnelly. "Then it was you told them."

"It was not. Do you think you can go around in New York like you was invisible? You take her to Gogo's place. Champagne—"

"There was no champagne!"

"Okay, so there was no champagne. Okay. It was Pop that seen you there."

"Pop, was it?" said Donnelly. "And it was Pop told Eddy and Moe?"

"That's right," said Nagle. "It was natural that he'd tell them. She is the same woman they saw over in Darby's hotel, and Eddy and Moe were good friends of Darby's."

"Sure it was natural," said Donnelly. "Only that Pop is in Buffalo."

Nagle made a slight move, a shift of the feet.

"Maybe he wrote them a letter."

"He would not write anybody a letter. And he did not see me at Gogo's place. He went to Buffalo last Thursday. You are a liar, Carlie."

"Now, look here, Marty—"

"If Eddy and Moe were talking, it was you told them, Carlie."

Something was happening, something was changing in the two men who did not move.

"I did not tell them," said Nagle.

"You are a liar," Donnelly said again. "If they were talking, it was you set them on to it. I'll never forgive it you."

"All right. They were not talking. I only told you that to make you see what you were doing. You can't keep this thing hid; you can't do it. They'll find out, and it's going to get them worried. You play around with this society bitch, and she gets you talking. Okay. One day you talk too much, and she turns you up. And the rest of us, too. For God's sake, Marty, drop her! You never let a woman throw you before. For God's sake, show some sense!"

"It's in your mind to set the others on her," said Donnelly.

"Then let her get the hell out of here. We—"

Donnelly struck, without any warning; his arm shot out straight from the shoulder, his fist caught Nagle on the point of the jaw, and sent him stumbling backward, with little running steps. He crashed into a chair and fell on the floor, with a thud that shook the house. As quick as a cat, Donnelly was on his knees beside him.

"Is he hurt?" Lucia asked, in a flat voice.

"No," said Donnelly. "Go back to your house."

He was bending over Nagle, and she moved, to see what he was doing.

"Marty . . . !" she cried. She tried to scream, but her throat contracted. "Marty . . ." she said, in a whisper.

"Be quiet!" he said, his teeth clenched. "Go home!"

She caught his arm, but it was like steel, like stone. His fingers were tight around Nagle's throat, and Nagle's pale eyes were bulging, his tongue showed between his gasping lips, his face was darkening.

"Marty . . ." she said, pulling at his arm with both hands. "Stop . . . I beg you . . . I beg you . . ."

She herself was choking. With her eyes fixed upon Nagle's awful face, she put her hands to her neck. She was choking and she was blind now, looking into blackness.

Donnelly lifted her onto the sagging couch. He raised her head and held a glass to her lips.

"Drink a little," he said. "It will help you."

The whisky had a rank, sour smell. She took a few sips; then she pushed the glass away, so violently that it fell out of his hand onto the floor.

"His glass . . ." she said.

She lay back, for a little time; then she sat up. Donnelly stood beside her, smoking a cigarette.

"As soon as you're able," he said, "go back to your house. Try now; can you get up?"

"Nagle . . . ?" she said, with a great effort.

"I will look after him."

"You killed him," she said. "You killed him. You choked him."

"I had to do it," he said.

"You killed him. You choked him—"

"Let you get back to your house now," he said.

"You killed him. You choked him—"

"Don't be saying that, darlin'," he said.

"How *could* you? How *could* you?" she demanded, beginning to cry.

"I had to do it. It was in his mind to set the two of them on you."

"Better . . ." she said. "Much better . . ." She was sobbing. "Anything—would be better—than that. Than *that*."

"Look!" he said, sitting down on the couch beside her. "It is hard for you, but you'll have to have courage. You'll have to stop crying. Suppose, now, somebody was to call you, and you'd have to go downstairs?"

"O God!" she cried, in despair.

No matter what happened to her, no matter how she felt, her first thought must always be, how to face her world. Her little world, her children, her father.

"I'd like some more whisky, please," she said. "Could I drink out of the bottle?"

"You could," he said. "Only go easy."

She took a few swallows.

"Have you a cigarette?" she asked.

He gave her one and lit it for her.

"Thank you," she said.

"You're welcome," he said.

They spoke with formality, as they had in the past. She smoked for a time, sitting up straight, growing quieter, growing stronger.

"What will you do—with him?"

"Leave it to me," he said. "Go back now to your house, and if they ask you any questions, tell them this. Tell them you'd invited me to take a cup of tea before I'd be off to Montreal. Then, while you were out this morning, Nagle comes, asking for me, and you sent him off to the boathouse to wait. Well, after a while you get to wondering is he still there, and you walk out, and you hear the two of us, having an argument. You wait awhile, and then you're off, leaving us at it."

"All right!" she said, frowning. "But what are you going to do with him?"

"Say it for me once, will you not?" he asked. "I mean, the way you'll tell it, if they ask you any questions."

"No. I'll remember."

"Say it once, will you not?"

"Oh . . . I'll say I asked you to tea, and Nagle came, asking for you, and I told him to wait in the boathouse, and I heard you having an argument. Now I want to know what you're going to do with him."

"I will take him in your boat and row off with him."

"That's ridiculous!" she said. "There are always lots of people out on the water, this time of day."

"I will manage," he said.

"Not that way. There's no place you could take him."

"I will leave him here, then, where he won't be seen, and I will come back for him later."

"Here? No. Can't you think of anything better than that?"

"I cannot," he said.

"Then I will. The—" She looked up at him, frightened to see him blurred and vague again. "Don't you realize the danger you're in?"

"I will manage."

"Your plans are—simply idiotic. If you're found with him, you won't have a chance. I'm sure any doctor would know how he'd been killed. You want me to tell people I left you having an 'argument' with him. I suppose you mean to swear you killed him in self-defense. Well, nobody would believe that. Not when you choked him."

"I will manage," he said.

He stood there, so big, so slow, so vague.

"You're a perfect fool!" she cried. "You've got to get him away. I'll bring my car to the door, and you—"

"I cannot drive," he said.

"Yes, you can. You drove me—"

"I cannot drive now," he said. "My arm has gone dead on me."

"What do you mean?"

"My arm," he explained. "I cannot use it at all."

She noticed then that his right arm hung limp at his side.

"You've got to use it," she said. "That's all just psychological."

"How's that?" he asked, anxiously.

"It's just imagination. You can use it."

"It is a judgment on me," he said.

"What!" she cried. "You *can't* be so ignorant and stupid. I'm going to bring the car here, and you've got to get him into it, and take him away. You've got to leave him somewhere, and then go home. Nobody ever needs know what happened to him. *Don't* be so spineless! Aren't you man enough to fight for your own life?"

"I cannot move my arm at all," he said. "It was done to me, so I could not get away. Go back to your house now—"

"You fool! You idiot! You coward!" she cried. "Snap out of it!"

He did not answer.

"Then I'll get you out of it," she said.

Chapter Eighteen

"Now look here!" she said. "I'll bring the car to the door and we—"

"No," he said. "I will not let you get into this."

"If you won't help me," she said, "I'll do it all alone. I'll get him down the stairs and into the car alone."

"Go back to your house," said Donnelly. "Leave me to manage my own way."

"I won't. You've got a chance, and you'll have to take it. I'll get the car, and you look around for something to—wrap him in."

"For the love of God, will you let me alone?" he cried.

"No. I won't. I'll do it all by myself if you're not man enough to help me."

"I will help you," he said, with an effort. He sighed, very deeply, and raised his head. "Have you a trunk, maybe?" he asked.

"Not here. But wait! There's that chest."

He looked where she pointed, at a long window seat, the top padded and covered with faded, moldering chintz. He went over to it and raised the lid.

"It will do," he said. "Only there are things in it, tools, and the like."

"Get them out," she said. "Oh, *try* to use your right hand . . . ! Here!"

She leaned over the chest, and brought out a trowel, two empty flashlight cases, a tangled mass of wire and rope and threw them on the floor; she was so fast, and he was so slow.

"Now we'll get him in," she said.

"You cannot!" said Donnelly, with a sort of horror.

"Oh, yes, I can!" she said.

"You don't know——"

"I picked up Rex—he was David's dog—I picked up Rex after he'd been run over. I carried him to the house," she said, proudly and arrogantly. "I can do anything I have to do."

"Not this," he said.

She turned then to look at Nagle. He was only a mound on the floor, covered with a dark green chenille tablecloth.

"Come on!" she said. "We've got to hurry."

Donnelly turned the chest over on its side.

"Hold open the lid," he said.

Using only his left arm, he pulled Nagle to the chest; he got him into it, lying on his back, with his knees raised high, because the chest was too short. He pushed the box upright, and Nagle shifted, with a faint thud..

"Now, while I'm getting the car," Lucia said, "do something with the tray and the whisky bottle. And the tools. Make the place look all right."

"I will," he said.

She ran down the stairs and opened the door. And out in the brilliant sunshine, terror seized her. Someone will see me, she thought. What can I say? What can I say?

She must not run. She must not look behind her. *Think!* Think of something to say to them. You must think.

She opened the garage door and got into the car. Think!

You can't get away with this. Someone is going to ask you where you're going. Someone will come to the boathouse. To see you and Martin dragging that chest down the stairs. What are you going to say?

She drove the car to the boathouse, and left the engine running when she got out. I *knew* I ought to save the gas, she thought. I knew something would turn up . . .

She opened the door, and saw Donnelly halfway down the stairs. He had wrapped the chest in the chenille cover and tied one end of it like the mouth of a sack; he held this in his left hand, letting the chest slide bumping down the steps ahead of him.

"That was a good thing to think of!" she said, pleased. "Now we'll get it into the car."

They could not. It was far too heavy for her, and he was of little use without his right hand.

"Can't you try?" she cried.

"God knows I would like to," he said.

They stood on the grass before the boathouse, with the chest at their feet, and they could not lift it into the car.

"Wait here!" she said. "I'm going to get Sibyl."

Sibyl was sitting in her neat, clean kitchen, reading a magazine. The sun was shining in, the wartime alarm clock ticked loudly.

"Sibyl," Lucia said, "help me, please. I've got to get a box into the car, and it's too heavy."

"Yes, ma'am," said Sibyl.

They walked to the boathouse, side by side.

"Mr. Donnelly's hurt his arm," Lucia said. "But I think we can manage, Sibyl."

It was very difficult, but they did manage. The chest was in the back of the car.

"Thank you, Sibyl," said Lucia. "You'd better get in front with me, Mr. Donnelly."

"*Mother!*"

It had happened. Bee was here, standing beside the car, her newly washed hair like silver in the sun.

"Mr. Donnelly wants to borrow an old engine I found in the boathouse," said Lucia. "He thinks he can fix it."

It was no trouble to say that. It was not necessary to think. The words simply came, when you needed them.

"But, Mother, where are you *going?*"

"To the station," said Lucia.

"But, Mother, Mrs. Lloyd'll be here—"

"Oh, I'll be back," said Lucia, carelessly.

"But, Mother, we can get a cab for—Mr. Donnelly—"

"No, dear," said Lucia. She started the car; they went down the drive and onto the highway.

"Holy Mother of God!" said Donnelly. "There was never another like you in the world."

"Can you think of any place to take the chest?"

"I don't know these parts at all."

"I don't, either," she said. "I haven't done any driving around. I suppose I'd better just go ahead . . . ?"

"You had. I'll keep my eyes open, for a lane or a byroad."

It's done, she thought. I got him out of it. She drove along, steadily, tranquilly, with an untroubled mind. The sweet air blew in her face; cars and trucks were rolling along the highway, each in its right lane, all so orderly. It's like riding in a procession.

It's done. I've got him out of it, the idiot. Sibyl will never say anything. Even if she knew . . . And maybe she does. I don't know. It doesn't matter. Anyhow, here he is.

Here he was, sitting beside her, riding along in the procession. The big parade . . . she said to herself. I got him out of it.

"You'd better really go to Montreal, right away," she said.

"I will," he said.

She glanced at him, and she did not trust him.

"You don't mean that," she said. "You haven't any intention of going to Montreal."

"I was just thinking . . ." he said, with humility.

A great pity for him rose in her. He was so helpless, so remote from her. He mustn't brood, she thought. I've got to get him talking.

There was only one thing in the world that *they* could talk about.

"Why did you come out here today?" she asked.

"Sibyl called me up. She told me Nagle was there."

"Why do you trust Sibyl so," she asked, "when you hardly know her?"

"It's a sort of idea I have," he said, with the same humility. "There's a kind of wisdom in her." He paused. "She is a realist," he said.

Strange word for him to use, she thought. Now he was silent again, and she did not like that.

"If you'd talk . . ." she said. "If we talked—about this . . ."

"I cannot talk at all," he said. "I'm sorry, but I cannot."

"We can't go on like this. We can't—just ignore it."

"I hope you'll forget it," he said. "Try, will you not?"

"Forget it?" she said, scornfully. "Not till the last day I live."

"I had to do it," he said. "You see, Carlie was a strange

man. He was a grand friend to the ones he liked, but there were not many of those. And if anyone did him a wrong, he'd never forget it. He was still talking about a teacher he'd had when he was a boy, over in Brooklyn. She's over eighty years of age now, but he was still trying to find a way to get back at her. He'd never have let up on you."

"But I never did him any harm!"

"He thought you did. He thought you wanted to break up the friendship there was between him and me."

There was a long moment's silence.

"There were other elements in it, too," he went on. "The first time he went out to see you, he came back very bitter. He was hurt."

"Hurt? That man?"

"He told me you looked down on him, you and your girl. He told me you were haughty to him. Like the dirt under your feet, he told me."

"I was afraid of him."

"Then you did not show it. Anyhow, he'd a great hatred for society women."

"*You* know better than to call me a 'society woman.' "

"It was the only word he had for it," said Donnelly, grave and gentle. "What they call 'the gentry,' in the old country. What he meant was, a woman with a standing in the world, a woman with a family, a good name. It was his conviction they'd always sell a man out, to keep what they had."

"He was a vindictive, ignorant man."

"Maybe," said Donnelly. "He always held it against his parents that they did not give him a good education, did not send him to college. They had him working for his father, that was a butcher, when he was fourteen, and it made him bitter. He was a smart man. It is a pity he did not get a good education."

"Did you—like him?"

"I did," he said.

"But—"

"I had to do it," he said. "Once he had an idea in his head, he'd never let go of it. And he gave himself away. He let me see what he had in his mind. If he'd set Eddy and Moe onto you, it would be the worst thing could ever happen to you."

"Why? What could they have done?"

"You would not understand, the way you've never met anyone like those two, and never will."

"Are they—gunmen?" she asked, timidly, afraid of hurting his feelings, but desperately curious.

"They are not," he said.

"But—what are they?"

"You would not understand."

"You could explain," she said.

"I will not," he said.

After a moment, he spoke again.

"There's a lane to the left," he said. "What do you think of it?"

She slowed down the car, and looked along the road that ran downhill from the highway, a pretty lane, with trees meeting overhead. There were no buildings to be seen, no traffic.

"We might try it," she said.

"We don't want to waste any time," he said.

"Why? Why do you say that?"

"You ought to be getting home," he said.

That's a strange thing to say, she thought, startled. A strange thing for him to be thinking, when there's this other thing . . .

Nagle is here, she thought, with a shock. In the car. In that chest.

She was driving along this quiet lane, with a dead man in the car, a murdered man. If the least thing went wrong, it would mean—God knew what. We can't do this! she thought. This is madness. We can't possibly get away with this.

She glanced at him. His head was turned away; he was looking into the woodland that bordered the lane. Think what could happen to him . . .

"Mr. Donnelly . . ." she said, a little loudly, "we've got to talk about this. We've got to have a plan, a story. It'll have to be self-defense."

"Oh, I'll think of a story," he said.

"We've got to have the same story, don't you see?"

"There's no need for you to be thinking about a story," he said. "No one's going to bother you about this."

"That's silly. Something could go wrong, any minute. You've got to think this out, carefully."

"I will."

"But now! Lieutenant Levy's been to see me already about—Ted Darby. He might very well come again, and ask questions. He—I think he's very clever."

"Lieutenant Levy? The police, is it?"

"The Horton County police. Suppose he goes into the boathouse? He might find something there—something we hadn't thought about?"

"Look!" Donnelly said. "There's a bit of a lake, around the bend of the road. You can see it from here."

The road was level now, along the floor of a little valley. She accelerated.

"Slow down!" he said, mildly. "There is a curve ahead."

And a car came around the curve, a roadster, with two soldiers in it.

"They saw us!" she said. "They could identify us!"

"Don't be nervous," said Donnelly. "You're trembling."

"Let's hurry!"

The engine backfired, and she gave a sort of scream.

"Don't! Don't!" he said, in distress.

It backfired again, and stopped, and started. Donnelly leaned forward.

"Your gauge is broken," he said.

"I know."

The car stopped. She pressed the starter, and nothing happened.

"I'll get out and crank it," she said.

"It will do you no good," he said. "You're out of gas."

"God damn it!" she cried.

"Don't! Don't!" he said. "It's not like you."

"What can we do? What in God's name can we do?"

"We are fine," he said. "We couldn't have found a better spot. Let you be easy now. Here! Have a cigarette!"

"There's a car coming!"

"Let it come. They'll see nothing at all but the two of us, having a little smoke."

"The chest!"

"People are taking around queer things in their cars, these days."

"Oh, *don't* you see? All these people can say they saw us here. After they've found—that."

"They will not find it. Smoke your cigarette now, and I'll tell you what we'll do."

I'm shaking, she thought. I wasn't, before. But this is the worst. Just to sit here, until someone gets us.

"We can't get away with this," she said.

"Wait, now!" he said. "Listen to what I'm saying, will you not? We can get away with this, if you'll do your part right. You'll have to pull yourself together."

"What can I do? What is there——?"

"Come!" he said. "We'll walk a little way, up the road."

"Leave—that?"

He got out of the car; he held out his hand, his left hand, to her; she took it, and got out beside him. Still holding her hand, he began to walk away.

"Listen now to what you've got to do," he said. "You've got to do it right. If you don't, we're sunk, the two of us. You've got to go home, as fast as you can."

"And leave you—like this?" she said. "I won't."

"Listen, will you not? Your girl said there was someone coming to visit you. Mrs. —" He paused a moment. "Mrs. Lloyd."

"How can you remember that?"

"I'm a good one for remembering. If you don't go home, your family'll be worrying. If you're away out of it too long, they'll have the police looking for you."

"Oh . . . !" she cried, angrily.

"You wouldn't want that," he said. "You'll have to get home as quick as ever you can. Here's how you'll do it. We passed a filling station on the highway, just a bit before we turned off here. It is not a long walk. Go there, and tell them to send for a taxi to take you to the railroad station.

Don't say anything about your car being stuck. You could give a kind of idea that the man you were driving with began to make trouble."

"I can't."

"Ah, you can!" he said. "Look how you answered your girl, quick as a flash. Now, when you get home— Are you paying heed to me?"

"Yes."

"Forget the story about us having an argument and all that. It will not do now. Here's the story you'll tell. Are you listening, dear?"

"Yes."

"Sibyl told you Nagle had come and she had sent him into the boathouse to wait. Well, you'd seen Nagle before and you did not like him much. You thought he had something to do with the black market. So you didn't hurry out to see him. You let him wait, hoping maybe he'd go away. Have you got that clear?"

"Yes."

"Then there's myself. Was there ever an old engine in the boathouse?"

"Yes."

"As soon as you've a chance, get rid of it. Throw it down into the water. Well, you'd told me I could take the engine, to see could I fix it. So, after your lunch, when you thought Nagle would be gone, you went out to the boathouse, to have a look at the engine. And, sure enough, Nagle is gone. You did not see him at all. Then I come along, and you say you'll give me a lift to the station. Well, we're driving along, and you ask me where am I taking the engine, and I tell you to a sort of a boat yard where a friend of mine is going to work on it. You'll remember all this?"

"Yes," she said, resisting every word of the story in her mind.

"Well, I have hurt my arm, and in the kindness of your heart, you say you will drive me to the boat yard. The gauge in the car is broke, and you don't know the gas is low until the car stops on you. When that happens, you know you've got to get home, or they'll be worrying. You leave the car with me, to go on to the boat yard, and you take the train."

"And what about you?"

"I'll wait a bit, till you're out of it. Then I'll go along to the filling station and telephone a friend of mine in New York. He'll drive out, and he'll bring gas for me. He'll help me with the chest, and we'll drive back to New York. Then I will get a late train to Montreal."

"No," she said.

"Now, what do you mean, at all?" he asked.

"I can't . . . How is your arm?"

"It is better."

"Can you move it now?"

"A little, I can."

"Let me see you," she said.

She was startled to hear him laugh.

"And what's so funny?" she demanded.

"The way you talk to me."

"I'm sorry," she said, coldly.

"I like it," he said. "Only, don't you be worrying about me. I've been looking after myself a good long while."

"I know," she said. "But . . ."

She remembered him in the boathouse, so helpless, so vague. It is a judgment on me, he had said.

"I'd like to see you move your arm," she said.

"Well, maybe I cannot, just now," he said. "It comes and goes. But whatever it is, it is passing off."

"Suppose the friend you're going to call up isn't home?"

"I've plenty of others."

"It'll be a long time, hours, before anyone can drive out here from New York."

"Well, I've a nice shady spot to wait in. I've cigarettes on me, and a bottle of whisky in my pocket."

"You mustn't *drink!*" she cried. "That'll make you do wrong, stupid things. You mustn't touch it!"

"I wouldn't take too much," he said. "But a drop of good whisky . . . I was thinking you'd take a little yourself, you're that pale."

A car was coming from the direction of the highway.

"O God! He'll go right past my car!" she cried.

"Let him," said Donnelly.

"But if he sees the car there, with no one in it, he might stop. He might get out, and look in the chest—"

"Now, why would he be doing that, dear? He won't stop at all. You want to remember this. There's no one else in the world knows what's in that box, and if you do your part right, there's no reason why anybody would ever know."

She wanted to stop until the car had passed, but he took her hand and led her on, toward the highway. When the car had gone, he dropped her hand, and reached into a breast pocket.

"Here's something you might be glad of," he said, and held out three little capsules, bright yellow.

"What are they?"

"They're little sleeping pills," he said. "One will do you. Swallow one of them, and you'll have a good night's sleep."

"Do *you* take things like that?"

"I do," he said.

"It's a terribly bad habit."

"I don't like to be lying awake," he said.

She dropped the capsules into the pocket of her dress, and he brought out a wallet from another breast pocket. He flipped it open, and leaning it against his chest, he drew out some bills.

"You're not using your right arm!" she said.

"You've no money on you," he said. "You'd better take this."

She put the bills into her pocket without looking at them. They were getting nearer to the highway now.

"Send me a wire from Montreal," she said.

"I will," he said. "And take it easy. There's nobody else in the world knows about Nagle. He won't be missed for a day or two, the way he moves around so much. And it'll be longer than that before ever he's found. When he is found —and maybe that'll never happen—he won't be in the box. Nobody'll know where he came to his end."

Now she could see a big green truck going along the highway.

"The filling station's only a bit of a way, to the left," he said. "You'll go home now—and you'll remember the story, will you not?"

"I can't," she said, stopping short. "I just can't. I'm—tired, or something. I can't go on."

From a side pocket he brought out a bottle of whisky.

"You've got to go home," he said. "You know that, don't you, darlin'?"

"Yes . . ." she said.

"I didn't drink from the bottle," he said, anxiously. "Nobody's touched it at all since you had a swallow."

She took a sip, and it seemed weak, almost tasteless. She went on, one sip after another.

"I wouldn't take any more," he said. "It'd make you drowsy, maybe. It is good Scotch, the real McCoy. You know what to buy, don't you?"

"It's my father's," she said.

And, in speaking his name, amazement overwhelmed her. I *can't* be drinking Father's whisky—here! she thought. This can't be true. Not possibly. Not possibly.

"Now you'll go home, will you not?" he asked.

"Yes . . ."

"You've saved my life this day," he said. "I'd lost my wits entirely. I'd never have got him out of the place, if you hadn't saved me."

You killed him for me, she thought. So that I'd be safe.

"To your left," he said. "It's not far."

"Yes . . ." she said. "Good-by. You'll—be careful, won't you?"

"I will that," he said. "Good-by now, and God bless you."

Chapter Nineteen

She could see the house now, through the taxi window. She was coming back just as she had left, hatless, in the red and white checked gingham dress; she had no purse with her, no powder, no mirror, no comb. She did not know how strange, how dreadful she might be looking.

It seemed to her completely beyond her strength to mount the few steps to the veranda. The cab drove off, and she did not move.

The door opened, and Bee came running down to her.

"Mother!" she cried, in an unsteady voice. "I've been almost crazy with worry. Mother, what were you *thinking* of? Mrs. Lloyd waited nearly an hour—"

"We ran out of gas," said Lucia.

"But why did you go at all? *Why* did you go off with that man?"

"I don't intend to answer any more questions," said Lucia.

"All right! Just think—how I feel! I gave Mrs. Lloyd tea—and I tried to talk to her." Bee was crying now. "I kept telling her—you'd be back any minute. I said—something must have happened to the car—and that's what I kept thinking. An *accident* . . ."

"I'm sorry you were worried," said Lucia, and moved forward. "But I'm tired now, Bee. I want to wash—"

"Mother, there's liquor on your breath! Mother, you've been *drinking!*"

She stood facing her mother, her eyes dilated, tears on her cheeks.

"Don't you dare to talk like that," said Lucia, evenly. "If I choose to take a cocktail now and then, I intend to do so. And don't you dare to call it 'drinking.' "

I drank out of a bottle, in a country lane, she thought. I must be let alone.

"Let me pass, please," she said. "I want to rest a little, before dinner."

"Lieutenant Levy's here!" said Bee.

Let me alone! Let me alone! Lucia cried to herself. She waited a moment.

"I'm too tired now," she said. "Ask him to come back tomorrow."

"You've *got* to see him, Mother," said Bee. "He's a policeman. You can't put him off."

"Certainly I can," said Lucia. "It's nothing important."

"Mother," said Bee, "you've made things queer enough, as it is. When Lieutenant Levy asked me when you were coming home, I couldn't tell him. *I didn't know where you were!*"

"Well, why should you always know where I am?"

"*Mother!*"

That word was like a wave, like a tide beating against her. Mother! Where have you been? What were you doing? Open your door, when I knock. Answer, when I ask. Be there, always, every moment, when I want you. It's—inhuman . . . she thought.

"I'll see Lieutenant Levy," she said, briefly. "Tell him I'll be down in a moment."

Her father came into the hall as she entered the house.

"Well, m'dear!" he said. "We were quite anxious—"

"Hello, Father!" she said, in a loud, cheerful voice, and went past him, up the stairs to her own room. She turned the key in the lock, and stood before the mirror.

She had thought of herself as bedraggled, grimy, pale, strange. But it was not so. Her hair was a little rough; there were faint smudges on her cheekbones, but, on the whole, she looked neat enough; a rather countrified housewife in a gingham dress.

She washed, and brushed her hair; she changed into a brown rayon dress with a ruffled peplum, ruffles on the sleeves. Fancy little number, David had called it, with disapproval. She did not like it herself, but what did it matter? She put on lipstick, more than usual, and, for some unrecognized reason, a necklace of green beads.

It's more about Ted Darby, she thought. I've just got to go through with it. Only, the whole Ted Darby episode seemed so far in the past, so unimportant. If it weren't for Father, she thought, I'd tell Lieutenant Levy the truth about it right now. There's nothing really horrible about it; nothing criminal.

Levy rose as she came into the room; he stood before her, tall, a little clumsy, with his big feet, his big nose, his big ears, yet with the mild, half-melancholy dignity that never left him.

"I'm sorry to bother you again, Mrs. Holley," he said. "But that's my job. I'm generally unwelcome."

"Oh, no!" Lucia said, warmly. "Not here! Smoke, if you like, Lieutenant."

"No, thank you," he said, and after she was seated, he sat down. "My housekeeper gives me a good idea of how hard things are for you ladies, these days," he said. "It must take the greater part of your day, just to get supplies."

"Well, you see, I have Sibyl," said Lucia. "She's wonderful."

"Does she do all the marketing?"

"Oh, I go sometimes," said Lucia. "But she's much better than I am."

"My housekeeper says you have to stick to one store, where they know you, if you want to get anything."

"Yes, you do," Lucia agreed.

I wish he'd get on with whatever he wants to ask, she thought. This is pretty boring.

But she appreciated his effort to establish a pleasant, easy atmosphere. It's the most sensible thing he could do, she thought, if he wants to get me talking, and off my guard. He had, she thought, a very good personality for disarming people, a slow, quiet voice, a gentle smile, a very courteous way of listening to every word you spoke. But she was on guard, and she would stay so; she would notice the first, the lightest change in his tone, in the drift of his talk.

He was talking on about his housekeeper; a Czech, she was, and a fine woman. She had been left a widow at twenty-five, in a strange country, with three children; she had brought them up, seen that they all got a good education. The two sons were in the Navy now; the daughter was married.

"But she keeps on working as hard as ever," he said. "The only thing that really upsets her is the shortage of soap. She was very apologetic about it, but she asked me to try, whenever I could, to get her a box of soap flakes. I haven't been able to find any of the three brands she wants, in spite of my exalted position." He smiled a little. "In one store they offered to sell me something called Silverglo. D'you think it would do?"

"Well . . ." said Lucia, "I don't think there's any real soap in it, but it seems to get things clean, and it's certainly easier to get."

"Silverglo . . ." he repeated, and reached in his pocket.

He's going to take notes about it, Lucia thought, amused.

"Is this yours, Mrs. Holley?" he asked, holding out a dirty little scrap of paper.

She did not want to take that paper into her hand. She looked at him, but she could read nothing in his face.

"Will you look at this, please, Mrs. Holley?" he asked.

She did not want to look at it. She was afraid. But that would be the worst mistake I could make, she thought. To say—I didn't want to look at it.

She took the paper, still with her eyes fixed on his face. Then, with heavy reluctance, she opened it. It was an old market list of hers. Mrs. Lloyd had told her about a market list found by Ted Darby's body. *This one?* she thought.

Or was this just a trap, something subtle and complicated, designed to make her talk? But he can't make me talk, she thought, and I won't lie, either. That's what he wants, for me to lie, and get all mixed up.

"Why, yes!" she said, as if surprised. "It's an old market list of mine. Where in the world did you find it, Lieutenant?"

"It was found under Darby's body," he said.

That's supposed to shock me, she thought.

"Good heavens! On the island?" she asked. "We went over there for a picnic, and I must have dropped it."

"I don't think so, Mrs. Holley. Your picnic was nearly two

weeks ago, and this paper hasn't been out in any rain."

"It looks as if it had," she said. "It's frightfully dirty."

"Mrs. Holley, can you tell me on what day you wrote this list?"

"Not possibly," she said. "There are things that are on almost all my lists. Oranges, whole-wheat bread—"

"You'll notice that the list says 'Try Silverglo?' Does that suggest anything to you, Mrs. Holley?"

"No, it doesn't," she said. "I often put that down about things."

"I have information that the first advertisement for Silverglo appeared in the newspapers on the sixteenth. Does that refresh your memory, Mrs. Holley?"

"Why, no. I'm sorry, but it doesn't."

She saw what it meant. The list could not have been written before the sixteenth, and Ted Darby's body had been found on the eighteenth.

"Can you suggest any way in which this paper could have got on the island, Mrs. Holley?"

"Why, no, Lieutenant. When I've finished with a list, I don't bother with it. I throw it away, just anywhere. It could blow away."

Over a mile, across the water, straight to Ted Darby's body?

"Or someone—anyone could pick it up," she said.

"Yes," he agreed, politely, and waited. But she said nothing.

"Mrs. Holley," he said, "I understand that you took out your motorboat, early on the morning of the seventeenth."

"I don't remember dates, Lieutenant, but it's possible. I often get up very early. I like to."

"Did you, on this occasion, see anyone on the island?"

"I didn't look at the island," she said, airily. "I just went scooting past."

"Mrs. Lloyd has made a statement," he said. "She states that early on the morning of the seventeenth, sometime between five and six, she saw a motorboat in the bay, with two women in it. She has the impression that the two women were engaged in some sort of struggle. Did you see this boat with two women in it, Mrs. Holley?"

Lucia was silent for a moment, seized by astonishment. Maybe I'd better say I did see two women in a boat, she thought. It might help me.

But she could not do that. Her astonishment was turning into a curious anger. You can't let people get away with things like that, she thought. Mrs. Lloyd just says anything that comes into her head, and she can't *do* that.

"If there'd been another boat out," she said, "I couldn't have helped seeing it, or at least hearing it. Well, there wasn't any. Mrs. Lloyd may be nearsighted. I stood up once, to button my coat. Perhaps that's what she saw."

"She seems very definite about what she saw, Mrs. Holley."

"But she's mistaken," said Lucia. "I *know* there wasn't any such boat, with two women in it. Not between five and six in the morning. I *know* it."

Looking at Levy's face, she felt a curious fear. He was grave and patient, but he was not convinced. But can't he see what Mrs. Lloyd is like? she thought. She's sweet, but she's featherbrained. I dare say she thinks she saw two women struggling in a boat—but she didn't. I *know* she didn't.

It came into her mind that things like this must happen sometimes during a trial. Suppose you were being tried for your life, she thought, and someone got up and made a statement like that? Suppose someone said—and really believed it—that they'd seen you in some place where you hadn't been? And maybe you couldn't prove you hadn't been there. Maybe all you could do was, to deny it.

She remembered David coming home from school one day, when he was a little boy.

"Miss Jesser said I scribbled in Petey's geography book," he had told her, pale, his eyes narrowed. "I didn't. But she won't believe me. I hate her! She's an old skunk!"

Lucia had gone to see Miss Jesser, but she had not been able to convince her.

"I don't want to make an issue of it, Mrs. Holley," she had said. "After all, it's not serious. At David's age, a child scarcely knows the difference between truth and falsehood."

Lucia had never been able to get any satisfaction for David. He had been falsely accused, and he had never been able to clear himself. Maybe he had forgotten about that—and maybe he had not. Maybe that happened to every child, at some time, leaving in every adult's mind the fear that she felt now, the fear of an utterly baseless accusation, coming like a bolt from the blue, and impossible to disprove.

"There wasn't any such boat," she said.

"Mrs. Holley," he said, "you understand that, no matter how reluctant I may be, it's my duty to enforce the law——"

"All laws?" she said. "Whether they're good or bad?"

"The laws in this country are made by the consent of the people. They can't be 'bad.' What the people decide for themselves is right, is, by that decision, right."

They were coming to something; she knew that. Everything they said was leading to a destined end. He was driving her—somewhere, and she had to resist.

"You don't care how unjust a law might be to an individual?" she asked, scornfully.

"The law isn't necessarily synonymous with justice, Mrs. Holley. After all, we don't know very much about justice. And we'd need wiser men than we're likely to get, to apply justice to everyone. What we have is a code, a written code, accessible to everyone."

"D'you think that's so wonderful?" she demanded.

"Yes," he said. "You wouldn't admit that even God had the right to punish or reward, if He never let anyone know what the laws were."

His words frightened her, and silenced her.

"Mrs. Holley," he said, "I suggest that your daughter was with you in the boat, on the morning of the seventeenth."

"My *daughter* . . . ?"

"Darby was not killed in the place where his body was found, Mrs. Holley. We're certain of that. We also know that Darby was in your boathouse at some time. We've found his fingerprints on several objects."

"Anyone could get in there. Anyone. But you said—you said Murray . . ."

"We've let Murray go, Mrs. Holley. One of the smartest criminal lawyers in New York came out last night to take his case—and it wasn't a very good case, anyhow. He's out now."

"But my daughter . . . Why are you trying to drag her into this?"

"Your daughter is attempting to shield you, Mrs. Holley.

That's obvious. I've questioned her, and she was extremely evasive."

"And what's she supposed to be shielding me from?" Lucia asked.

"Mrs. Holley, it's my duty to inform you that you are not obliged to answer my questions. It is furthermore my duty to inform you that anything you say may——"

"Don't *talk* like that!" she cried.

He rose, and stood before her, and he was so immensely, toweringly tall that she could not see his face.

"Mrs. Holley. I have evidence that Darby was in your boathouse. I have good reason to believe that he was killed there and his body later removed to the island. I have reason to believe that this afternoon Donnelly assisted you to remove from the boathouse some object or objects which you feared might tend to incriminate you."

"No," Lucia said. "No, I didn't."

"I haven't applied for a warrant, Mrs. Holley——"

"A warrant?" she cried. "For—me?"

"I'd certainly be justified, Mrs. Holley, in holding you, and your daughter for questioning. You're both withholding information."

"My daughter . . . ?"

"Your daughter is very evasive, Mrs. Holley. She told me that Donnelly had come here to see her. She gave me to understand that he was infatuated with her, and was attempting to win your good will, for that reason. Further questioning made it plain that she knows nothing at all about the man. She doesn't know his first name, for instance, or his address. She 'can't remember' where or when she met him. She then told me the same story about Darby.

That if he had come here at any time—which she didn't admit—it was to see her." He paused. "How long have you known Donnelly, Mrs. Holley?"

"Oh, not long. He's—just an acquaintance."

"How did you make his acquaintance, Mrs. Holley?"

"Well, I *think* some life-insurance agent introduced him."

"Do you know what Donnelly's occupation is, Mrs. Holley?"

"No," she said. "No, I don't."

"He was arrested five times in connection with bootlegging and rumrunning, during prohibition. At present, the O.P.A. is interested in him. There's good reason to believe that he's active in the black market, particularly in meat."

"But he hasn't done anything really—criminal, has he? I mean, robbery, or——?"

"Mrs. Holley," said Levy, "your attitude is surprising. If you don't consider black market activity, in wartime, a criminal offense——"

"I *do!*" she said, quickly. "Of course I do!"

"Mrs. Holley," said Levy, "I shall have to ask you what you and Donnelly removed from the boathouse this afternoon."

She sat very still. She did not realize that she was holding her breath until it burst out in a faint gasp.

"An engine," she said. "An outboard motor."

"That's what your daughter told me," he said. "When I asked her where you were, she told me you'd driven Donnelly to the station, taking with you an outboard motor. I made an opportunity to visit the boathouse, and the engine is still there."

"There were two."

"Did the landlord give you an inventory of the contents of the boathouse, Mrs. Holley?"

"Yes. Yes, I think so. But I don't exactly remember where it is. I can *find* it, of course, later on . . ."

"Why did you put the engine in a chest, Mrs. Holley?"

"Well, I always like to put things in boxes . . ."

The end of the tether, she said to herself. You go as far as you can, and then the rope is stretched tight and you can't go on.

"Where did you take this chest, Mrs. Holley?"

"Well, we were going to take it to a boat yard, but we ran out of gas, and I came home by train."

"Where did you leave Donnelly?"

"In the country. In a lane."

"What part of the country?"

"I don't know exactly."

"What station did you take the train from?"

"It was—I think it was called West Whitehills."

"When is Donnelly going to return your car, Mrs. Holley?"

"Well, very soon, I guess."

"I'll have to question Donnelly, Mrs. Holley. Will you give me his address, please?"

"I haven't got it."

"How do you communicate with Donnelly, Mrs. Holley?"

"Well, I don't."

"Has any member of your family his address?"

"No. I'm sorry."

"Mrs. Holley, I suggest that you and Donnelly removed evidence pertaining to Darby's death."

"No! Really we didn't. I promise you we didn't."

You get to the end of the tether, but nothing happens. The rope doesn't break; it doesn't choke you to death.

"I can't accept your story about this engine, Mrs. Holley. You've given me no satisfactory explanation for the presence of your market list under Darby's body. Neither you nor your daughter has given me any plausible explanation for Darby's presence in your boathouse. I'll have to ask you to come with me to the District Attorney's office."

"Well, but—when?"

"Immediately."

"But it's almost dinnertime!"

"I'm sorry."

"But—when would I get back? I mean, what time shall I tell Sibyl to put dinner on?"

"I don't know, Mrs. Holley."

"An hour?"

"It would be better not to count on that, Mrs. Holley."

"You mean . . . ? You don't mean—they'd keep me?"

"That's a possibility, Mrs. Holley."

"You mean—arrest me?"

"I think it's a possibility that the District Attorney may consider it advisable to hold you for further questioning."

"Hold me? In prison?"

"It's a possibility, Mrs. Holley."

"I can't," she said, flatly. "I can't possibly just walk out of the house like this, and go to prison. You don't realize . . . I've got my children and my father . . . Perhaps you didn't know that my husband's overseas, in the Navy?"

"Yes. I knew that, Mrs. Holley."

"Then don't you see . . . ? Don't you see what it would do to them all? I *can't* . . . Don't you see? They can't—just sit down to dinner . . ."

She rose; she clasped her hands, to keep from seizing his sleeve.

"Please!" she said. "You understand human nature. You *know* I didn't kill Ted Darby. You don't want to bring such disgrace and misery—to all of us—"

"Mrs. Holley," he said, "you've been consorting with a known criminal—"

" 'Consorting'?" she repeated, looking into his face.

"That's the usual expression," he said, returning her look steadily.

He thinks we're lovers, she told herself. Everyone will think so. The police will find out about that lunch. About everything.

But nobody knows anything about Nagle; maybe they never will. Maybe if I tell the truth about Ted Darby now, it will be the end. Only I've got to warn Father.

"Lieutenant Levy," she said. "Let me have until tomorrow morning. I beg of you."

"It's not possible, Mrs. Holley."

"I'm—so tired," she said. "I can't put things very clearly. If I can just have a good night's sleep, then tomorrow I'll—tell you."

"Tell me what, Mrs. Holley?"

"About Ted Darby," she said.

"You admit that you know the circumstances of his death?"

"Please," she said, "please just let me have until tomorrow morning."

"That's impossible, Mrs. Holley."

"It has to be that way," she said.

Because I won't let them spring it on Father, she thought. It'll be hard enough for him, no matter how careful I am about telling him. He doesn't even know that the man he met in the boathouse was the horrible Ted Darby he read about in the newspapers. He'll—

"Mrs. Holley," said Levy, "I don't think you understand your position. It's extremely serious. You've admitted that you have knowledge of Darby's murder—"

"It wasn't a murder."

"Of Darby's death. By admitting this knowledge, Mrs. Holley, you've rendered yourself liable to arrest."

"Look!" she said, with desperate earnestness. "Lieutenant, let's just talk, like—people. You *know* I'm not a murderess. I should have told you the whole thing before, but I had a reason—it seemed to me a good reason. I'll tell you everything tomorrow morning. As early as you like."

"Why not now?"

"I need a good night's sleep. I'm—really, I'm so tired . . ."

He moved away, his hands clasped behind his back.

"Mrs. Holley," he said, after a moment, "I'll postpone questioning you any further until tomorrow, if you'll get Donnelly here tonight."

Chapter Twenty

She walked over to the window, and she was startled to see how it looked out there in the world; everything bathed in a clear lemon light; the coarse grass looked yellow, the leaves on the young trees were a translucent green, and trembling strangely in the strange light.

He's gone now, she told herself. He's on the train, going to Montreal.

But in her mind she could see him only in the lane, as she had left him, tall and neat, his right arm hanging useless by his side. And that's the bargain, she thought. I'm to sell him out. I'm to get him here, and hand him over to the police.

There were footsteps overhead; a door closed. Father, she thought. I suppose Bee's upstairs, too. And David? It's nearly time for dinner.

"Mrs. Holley?"

Levy's tone was courteous and patient; too patient. It's ridiculous for him to wait like this, she thought, with a sudden anger, when he could make me give him an answer.

"I don't know where Mr. Donnelly is," she said, evenly.

"Then I'm afraid we'll have to be getting along, Mrs. Holley."

"You can let me have my dinner, can't you?"

"I'm afraid not."

She turned to face him. The room was growing shadowy, and that made him look very pale, his hair very black.

"I didn't think *you'd* behave like this," she said.

He said nothing.

"Why don't you find Mr. Donnelly for yourself?" she demanded. "If you're so anxious to see him."

"I've tried. But the New York police have lost track of him, temporarily. They'll trace him, of course, but I'd like to see him now."

"You'll arrest him, won't you?"

"I want to question him, Mrs. Holley. If his answers are satisfactory, he'll have no further trouble."

He's been arrested five times, Lucia thought. And they never could convict him. He knows how to look after himself. And they won't ask him about Nagle. Why should they? Nobody can know yet that anything's happened to Nagle. The rest of it isn't dangerous for him. Lieutenant Levy will only ask him about Ted Darby, and he can easily clear himself. He must have an alibi for that evening; certainly he wasn't here.

And about the chest? He'll certainly have got rid of that, long ago. And nobody can possibly know about Nagle yet. No. Martin will say what I said. That it was an engine. He'll be able to answer all Lieutenant Levy's questions—much better than I can. He's been arrested five times, and they couldn't hold him. *He* knows how to look after himself.

She heard the screen door in the kitchen bang, and David's voice, loud and hearty.

"Hello, Sibyl! What's with dinner?"

"Lieutenant Levy's talking to your mother just now," Sibyl answered, in her gentle voice.

"Aha!" said David, pleased. "He's a smart cooky. I bet he cracks this case. Any coke in the icebox, Sibyl?"

"No, Master David. Can't get any."

"Well . . ." said David. "Maybe I'll mix up a chocolate malted."

"Spoil your appetite!"

"It never does," said David.

"I'll mix it for you," said Sibyl.

All the little sounds were strikingly clear to Lucia. That was the bowl being set down on the kitchen cabinet; here was the egg beater clattering, and catching, and starting again. David, she thought, would be sitting on the edge of the kitchen table, happy to be home.

I can't spoil this for David. For all of them. I *will not* go off now, just at dinnertime, to the District Attorney's office. And maybe not come back tonight—not for days. And let them hear—let everyone hear—that I consorted with a known criminal . . .

I'd do anything, to keep that from happening.

He would keep it from happening, if he came. He'd know how to answer Lieutenant Levy, and the District Attorney. He'd know how to help me out of this, if he came. He'd put that first.

"Mrs. Holley, I'll have to have your decision," said Levy.

The egg beater had stopped; she heard the oven door open and shut.

"Yes . . ." she said, and went out of the room, along the hall to the kitchen.

"Hello, David, dear!" she said. "Sibyl, will you come into the sitting room for a moment, please?"

"Sibyl's going to be grilled, is she?" asked David. "Well, watch your step, Sibyl!"

Sibyl smiled at him softly, and followed Lucia back to the sitting room.

"Sibyl," said Lucia, "do you happen to know Mr. Donnelly's telephone number?"

Sibyl looked at her; their eyes met. If she said no, that would be fate.

"Yes, ma'am," said Sibyl.

"You might call him now," said Levy. "Say that Mrs. Holley would like him to come out this evening, as early as possible. Don't mention me."

"No, sir," said Sibyl.

The telephone was on a little table in the hall, just outside the sitting-room door; they could both see her as she sat down on the chair and dialed. Her face looked composed and sorrowful, with her eyes lowered. She's dialing a wrong number, Lucia thought. She likes Martin, and she knows this is a trap for him.

"Hello?" said Sibyl. "May I speak to Mr. Donnelly, please? . . . You expect him in soon? Well, will you please tell him Sibyl says will he please come out to see her this evening, soon as he can? Thank you, sir."

"He's not home, ma'am," she said, rising. "But I left a message."

"With whom?" asked Levy.

"Don't know who it was, sir."

"You might give me the number, please," said Levy, and Sibyl repeated a number which he wrote down in a notebook.

It's a wrong number, Lucia thought. Sibyl wouldn't do this to Martin.

Anyhow, he's gone now. He's on the train now, going to Montreal. He's not coming here. He's gone.

"Thanks," said Levy, putting the little book back into his pocket. "Then I'll see you tomorrow, Mrs. Holley. Good night!"

"Good night!" Lucia answered.

As soon as the door had closed after him, Lucia hurried to the kitchen, almost breathless with impatience to hear what Sibyl would have to say.

"Sibyl . . . ?"

"Yes, ma'am?"

Their eyes met, and Sibyl's were unfathomable, dark, sorrowful and steady.

"Sibyl . . . Do you think he'll come?"

"Left the message, ma'am."

But did you, really? Lucia thought. Or did you just pretend to? You like him. Would you really get him out here —for a policeman?

She stood looking at Sibyl, and she could not ask her that question.

Anyhow, he's gone. He's on the train to Montreal.

"Shall I ring now, ma'am?"

"I suppose so," said Lucia.

She thought that Sibyl enjoyed sounding the gongs in the hall, a series of four strung on a red silk cord; an old thing, that had belonged to Lucia's mother. David and Bee had loved the chimes in their childhood; it was a part of their family life; they had brought it along as a matter of course.

The setting sun made a gold dazzle on the glass of the front door, but the brilliance did not reach Sibyl; she stood in shadow, with the little padded wooden stick in her hand. She struck the lowest and deepest gong, and went on, up to the fourth, then down, then up once more; the notes hummed through the house. And it was like a charm; old Mr. Harper at once came out of his room, then David opened his door; before they had reached the hall, Bee was coming down the stairs.

I want Tom here! Lucia said to herself, in passionate rebellion. I want them all here, all safe. It was an impious wish, a rebellion against heaven, against life itself. She knew that. But she would try, she would fight, to turn away the tide from her doorstep.

She felt that she could do anything. She could sit at the table, she could even eat a little. That was because she had set a limit to her ordeal.

At nine o'clock, she told herself, I'll say I'm tired, and I'll go upstairs. And I'll take one of his pills and go to sleep.

Bee and David were 'queer'; she noticed that at once. They were unusually silent; they were disapproving of her. Let them. They would get over it. Her father talked, and she responded, soothed by his kindly vagueness. He had never disapproved of her. If he had noticed any of her strange goings-on lately, or if anyone were to tell him of still stranger goings-on, he would dismiss it all. She was his daughter; she was the irreproachable wife and mother, the wise and prudent housekeeper. The worst he would ever admit against her was, that perhaps she had been somewhat lacking in judgment.

But her husband and her children did not consider her beyond criticism. She belonged to them; whatever she did affected them; their pride, their good name in the world lay in her hands. They would give her love, protection, even a sort of homage, but in return for that she must be what they wanted and needed her to be.

They all went into the sitting room after dinner. Bee sat

down at the desk to write a letter; David took up a science magazine; old Mr. Harper proposed a game of cribbage. It was only a little after eight, but Lucia could not keep to her self-imposed limit of nine o'clock.

"Father," she said, "if you don't mind, I think I'll just write to Tom, and then go to bed."

"Very good idea!" he said. "Have you anything to read, m'dear? I have this book from the lending library, very amusing; light touch. This family in a cathedral town in England—"

"I'm sure I'd like it, Father, but I don't think I'll read anything tonight. I think I'll go right to sleep. Good night, Father. Good night, children."

David rose, and kissed her cheek; it was a stern kiss, but at least he accepted her.

"Good night, Mother," said Bee, not even raising her head from her writing.

You're unkind, Lucia thought. But that's because it's much, much harder for you than it is for David. He just thinks I'm being silly and trying, but you feel that there's something more, something dreadful, and you're frightened. I'm sorry . . .

It was necessary to write Tom's letter quickly, while she could. Her room was tranquil in the lamplight; a soft salt wind blew in at the open windows.

Dear Tom.

It was as if something stirred behind a curtain.

Dear Tom. The weather. Dear Tom. Oh, Tom, *come alive!* Be real. Let me remember how you were, let me see you. Let me feel something about you. Anything. You mustn't, you can't be this far away, so that you're not real.

But there was no feeling in her, for anyone. She was in

a hurry to get to sleep, that was all. Folded in the back of the writing tablet she found an old letter to Tom that had not seemed good enough to send. She copied it, almost without change. There were little domestic details; there was a reminder of a day they had spent together at Jones Beach, long ago, when the children were little. It had been a special day, specially happy, but it evoked no feeling in her now. That young, happy Tom and Lucia were no more than bright little dolls.

She addressed the envelope and stood it up against Tom's picture, where every night an envelope stood. She had wrapped the yellow capsules in a paper handkerchief and put them into a bureau drawer. She took one out now, and swallowed it with a glass of water. I don't even know what it is, she thought. I don't know what it will do to me.

Only it would do her no harm. She was not afraid of anything from his hands. She undressed, and bathed, hurrying, for fear sleep would suddenly overcome her. I might fall down, she thought; I might fall asleep just anywhere, and in the morning, they'd find me on the floor. How long will it last, I wonder? So that they'll have trouble waking me up in the morning?

It worried her to think of that, of being drugged and 'queer' in the morning. Especially when I've got to tell Father about Ted, she thought. But nothing really mattered except getting through this night, sleeping through it, utterly unconscious. There's nothing to stay awake for, she thought. It's out of my hands now. I let Sibyl give that message. But he won't come. He's on his way to Montreal now.

She got into bed and lay there, propped up on two pillows, the lamp still lighted. She took up a book, but that was no good. What's the matter with that pill? she thought, impatiently. Why doesn't it start? I'll give it twenty minutes more, and then, if nothing's happened, I'll take another.

She closed her eyes, and a face was forming before her; she watched it anxiously. It was a familiar face, bony, wearing pince-nez, and a simpering smile. Now, who's that? she thought. I ought to know. Why, yes; it's Miss Priest, our English teacher. But didn't I hear from someone that she'd died? Well, has she come to give me a message?

"Miss Priest?" she asked, apologetically.

No answer. Lucia sighed, and put the pillows down flat; she stretched out her legs, relaxing. Miss Priest, she thought, trying to remember something. About school, was it? I don't care whether I actually sleep or not, she thought, as long as I can relax like this. And not worry.

Sibyl's voice was hissing in her ear.

"I'm asleep!" Lucia said, angrily. "Let me alone!"

Hiss, hiss, hiss. Misss-ess Holley.

"Let me alone, Sibyl."

"Mrs. Holley, he's here, ma'am. Got to hurry."

Holley. Here. Hurry. Hiss, hiss, hiss.

Sibyl laid a cold, wet washcloth across her forehead, drew it across her eyes.

"Again!" Lucia said.

She opened her eyes and sat up.

"Got to hurry, ma'am. He's here."

"I can't hurry, Sibyl. I took a pill. I was asleep."

"I'll help you, ma'am."

This was a dreadful way to feel, so leaden, so confused. And so indifferent. She sat in a chair while Sibyl put on her shoes and stockings and pinned up her hair.

"What time is it, Sibyl?" she asked.

"Nearly two o'clock, ma'am."

Lucia began to cry a little.

"I didn't get to sleep until after nine," she said. "I haven't had—enough sleep."

"You can go back to sleep later, ma'am."

The dimly lit hall frightened her; she held back, in dread that one of those closed doors would open. But Sibyl took her hand and led her to the stairs; she went down carefully, on wooden feet, still holding Sibyl's hand. They went through the dark kitchen and out onto the back porch, and it was black as pitch there.

"It's raining!" she whispered.

"Just a little bit, ma'am," Sibyl whispered back. "Got to be very quiet now, ma'am."

There was a man moving along the drive; Lucia saw the dull gleam of his raincoat as he passed within a few feet of them.

"Now!" Sibyl whispered.

They went, half running, across the grass, to the boathouse. Sibyl opened the door and they entered, and it was pitch-dark in there, and there was a cold, musty smell.

"This way, ma'am," Sibyl said.

She opened the door that led to a little pantry without a window, and the light from the unshaded bulb that hung from the ceiling was dazzling. He was there.

"It was kind of you to come," he said, with formality.

This was not a dream, and she was not leaden and drowsy now. He was most immaculately neat, in his dark suit and dark tie, his arm in a black sling; he was not blurred now, but sharp and clear. He was completely a stranger to her, and she was cold with fear at the sight of him.

This brilliant little room without a window was a trap, that she had got him into. And now she was shut up in it with him. This was the meeting that she had dreaded more than anything in the world.

"I wouldn't have bothered you," he said, "only my arm is broke on me."

"Broken?" she cried.

"Broken," he repeated, apologetically. "If it wasn't for that, I'd have mailed you the things, with a bit of a note, to explain. Only the way it is, I cannot write."

"Have you had your arm set?"

"That'll come later. Look, will you, what's on the shelf?"

"You can't go on like this! It must hurt you—horribly."

"I don't think of it," he said. "Don't worry. It'll be cared for, later. Look, now, what's on the shelf."

But she kept her eyes upon his face, that had so strangely gay a look.

"Look, now!" he said. "Here's your girl's letters, every last one of them."

He picked up from the drainboard a little bundle of envelopes in an elastic band.

"You'll have no more worry about them," he said. "And here . . . Won't you look? Here's your jewels." He smiled a little. "They're not so grand as I'd been thinking."

"Martin . . ." she said.

The dam was giving way, the great wave was mounting, to engulf her.

"Martin," she said, "your arm is broken. Martin, you must get away, quick."

"There's no great hurry."

"There is! There is! There's a policeman—"

"He is just patrolling. I saw him before, and I kept out

of his way while I knocked on the kitchen window and Sibyl came out."

"Martin . . . I'll take you in the rowboat—farther down the shore. Hurry! You must hurry! The policeman might come here."

"He wouldn't be bothering with me."

"But that's what he's here for! I'll take you in the rowboat. I'll get you away, somehow."

"The cop's not looking for me."

"But, Martin! Lieutenant Levy knows about the message——"

"What message?"

He doesn't know, she thought. And if he finds out . . .

"What message was it?" he repeated. "I want the truth of it."

He was looking at her, in a narrow, thoughtful way, as if he were making up his mind. She could not speak; she could not turn her eyes away from him.

"You sent me a message?" he said. "What was it?"

He waited a moment.

"So that's the way of it?" he said. "You turned me in."

"Martin . . ." she said.

He gave a long sigh.

"Ah, well . . ." he said. "That's what poor Nagle meant, y'know."

Chapter Twenty-one

She could not understand the words; only the tone, that had in it no trace of bitterness or reproach.

"You could not help it," he said. "Levy got after you, did he?"

"It was only about Ted Darby," she said. "He doesn't know about anything else. He only thinks we took something away—evidence—about Ted. Nothing else. Nothing —that could really hurt you. I wouldn't—you know I wouldn't . . . Never about—the other. Never!"

"My poor girl," he said, "you couldn't help yourself at all. That's what Nagle meant, y'know. A woman like yourself will always have to be thinking of her family and her good name first."

"No. Not about—the other. I'd never give you away. Never!"

"Sure, I believe you," he said.

"You don't. I can see that you don't. You think——"

"Look, now! Would I forget the way you helped me get him out, in that chest? Would I forget the courage you had, and the spirit, answering your girl as quick as a flash? You've been good to me."

"No," she said. "I haven't."

"Well, I'm satisfied," he said, with a flicker of that strange gaiety. "Sit down now, will you not? There's a few things—"

"No! You've got to get away now—this instant—in the rowboat."

"You will have to listen, my poor girl," he said, "for my mind is made up."

"You must go!" she said.

"There's no chair in it," he said, glancing around the pantry. "Well, I'll be quick. There's no one ever need know Nagle was in the chest, and the chest itself is burned to ashes. You've only to say you don't know what I had in the chest at all, or where I took it."

"Where is Nagle?"

"It's better you don't know that. Anyhow, he is far from here, and there's nobody knows he was ever in the boathouse but the two of us, and Sibyl. Your car's in the garage by the station. I sent a young boy with it. There's nothing to tie you with Nagle."

"And what about *you*? What are *you* going to do?"

"I can't get away with it," he said, "if the cops are looking for me here."

"You can! I'll take you in the rowboat."

"No," he said, "I can't get away with it. And well I knew it, from the start."

"Martin, even if they did catch you tonight, they'd only ask you questions about Darby. They don't know about Nagle."

He took out a pack of cigarettes and shook one into his hand.

"Will you give me a light, please?" he asked. "It is hard—"

"Aren't you *going*?"

"A few drags . . ." he said, apologetically. "It is a comfort."

She struck a match and held it out for him.

"Martin," she said, "you're not being—sensible. You *can* get away. If I take you in the rowboat——"

"I'll not go in the boat with you," he said.

"Then go by the road. We'll watch, Sibyl and I, until the policeman's on the other side of the house, and then you can get away."

"Sure!" he said, absently, drawing on the cigarette.

"Martin!" she cried. "You've got something in your mind! Something silly."

"A life for a life," he said. "That's the way of it."

"It doesn't have to be—unless you just give up. Martin, aren't you man enough to fight for your life?"

"There are things you can't fight," he said. "Carlie and I, we were friends for near twenty years. It never came into his head I'd do that to him. Surprised, he looked, like——"

"Stop! Don't talk like that! You——" She stopped for a moment, appalled by the look on his face, the blankness. "Don't be a fool! Pull yourself together. You've got to fight for your life."

"And what kind of life would it be at all, with never a moment's peace, day or night? I'd never lay my head on my pillow that I wouldn't see Carlie——"

"Shut up!" she said, furiously. "You did it for me."

"That was the same as doing it for myself," he said. "There is no merit in that."

"Snap out of it! You can get away—if you'll stop being such a dope."

He was looking down at her with a smile.

"Stop that smiling!" she said. "There's nothing to smile about. For God's *sake*, will you pull yourself together and *think*?"

"I will," he said, readily.

"And you'll go to Montreal?"

"I will try."

"Don't say that. Don't think that way. Say you will go to Montreal."

"I will," he said.

"I don't trust you! You've got something in your mind. You think that because I sent—because I had to send that message—you think it's fate, or something."

"It is not fate I believe in," he said.

She was silent, in a furious effort to find the right words, to reach him, to rouse him.

"Martin," she said, "you've managed so well, up to now. You've burned the chest; you've—managed everything. You won't go to pieces now, when the worst of it's all over?"

"Oh, I won't," he said. "Don't you be worrying, dear."

"Martin, you don't—you can't believe—what Nagle said . . . ?"

"I do not," he said.

She was leaning against the drainboard, supporting herself with one outstretched hand. He laid his hand over it.

"Good-by now," he said.

"Martin . . ."

But he had opened the door and gone into the dark room beyond. She moved after him, groping, lost in the blackness. The front door closed softly.

"Sibyl?" she called, sharply.

"Yes, ma'am?"

"We ought to—"

Ought to do what? She made her way across the room and opened the door. It was lighter out there, and she saw Donnelly moving quickly across the grass, going toward the highway. Then a flashlight swung in a half circle, and she shrank back against the house.

Now there would be a shout. Now there would be a shot.

The flashlight swung again, and she had a glimpse of stunted bushes that seemed to slide along the beam of light. The water lapped softly against the boathouse; the rain made a whispering sound.

"Now, ma'am?" said Sibyl, close to her ear.

It was a dreadful thing, to cross that dark, open space. The flashlight would catch them, and they would be paralyzed by it; they would stand frozen.

It was a dreadful thing to go up the stairs. A door would open, a voice would call to her.

"I'll help you get to bed, ma'am."

"No, thank you, Sibyl. No, thank you."

Her own lamplit room was not safe. Someone could knock; someone could open the door. She undressed in frantic haste, and threw all her damp clothes into the closet; she put on her pajamas and lay down on the bed.

She lay very still, waiting for the shot to ring out, for the sound of footsteps running up the stairs.

Chapter Twenty-two

She waked in a gray twilight, and looked at her watch. It was half-past four. That's too early, she said to herself, and frowned, worried by the words. What was it about 'too early'? Something important. Too early . . .

Come as early as you like tomorrow morning, she had told Levy, and this was tomorrow morning. I'll have to talk to Father first, she thought, but not just yet. I can sleep a little longer.

She had a dream, about Sibyl. Sibyl was living in a little shack, by the edge of a swamp, and the sheriff and his men were coming to get her husband. But that was all right, because she knew it was only a dream. The swamp was a dream swamp, a jungle of tall, dark trees festooned with strange white moss that rustled like paper. The sheriff and his men had brought bloodhounds with them, and they went into the jungle-swamp, splashing through water. She could not see them now, but the hounds began to bay, and it froze her blood.

She heard a high, squealing whistle. That's a bazooka gun! she thought. Oh, Tom, be careful! Now she knew that it was Tom in the gloomy swamp, hunted by dogs, and his leg was broken. She tried to run to him, and she could not stir; she tried to call to him, and her voice was strangled. Some gasping little sound came, and waked her.

There was the same gray twilight in the room, and the house was very quiet. But it was after seven, by her watch. I'll have to talk to Father, she thought, and got up. A sick dizziness came rushing up, spinning round and round, from her feet into her head; she fell back on the bed, and the bed rose from the floor and spun, in a great swoop.

When that stopped, she was afraid to move, for fear it would start again. She still felt sick, and too tired, too weak to lift her head. I can't talk to Father, she thought. I can't get up. They'll have to let me alone for a little while, until this goes away.

There was a knock at the door, and Sibyl came in with a tray. She set the tray down, and came over to the bed; she helped Lucia to lie back against the pillows; she drew the sheet neatly up over her chest.

"Thought you'd like some breakfast, ma'am."

"Sibyl . . . Have you heard anything?"

"No, ma'am."

"Did you look in the newspapers?"

"Yes, ma'am. There's nothing."

"Sibyl, I'd like to rest for a while."

Sibyl poured her a cup of coffee.

"If you'll just tell the others that I'm tired, and that I'd like to rest until lunchtime . . . If you'll just see that no one disturbs me, Sibyl . . ."

"I'll tell them, ma'am," said Sibyl, with no spark of hope.

"Can't you see to that for me?" Lucia demanded, ready to cry.

"I'll tell them, ma'am. That's all I can do," said Sibyl.

There was nothing sympathetic in her tone; her face was

completely inexpressive. Tears were running down Lucia's cheeks as she drank her coffee. Sibyl's absolutely heartless, she told herself. She could see that I got a little peace and quiet, if she wanted.

The coffee made her feel better. No, she thought, Sibyl's not heartless. She's a realist, that's all. She knows you have to do things. I'll lie here until Lieutenant Levy comes. Then he can wait downstairs until I've talked to Father. He can just wait. Do him good.

She drank two cups of coffee, and lit a cigarette. But it was curiously bitter, and she put it out. I really don't feel at all well, she thought. I think I'm on the verge of a breakdown. What, exactly, was a breakdown? Aunt Agnes had a nervous breakdown. Lots of people do. Maybe this was it, this bodily weakness and weariness, this refusal of the mind to think or to feel. This is how sick animals feel, she thought. When Tom's collie was sick, he always wagged his tail when Tom spoke to him. I used to think he hated to do it. Toward the end, he didn't even open his eyes; just gave one little thump with his tail. Because he felt he had to, on Tom's account. I always thought he didn't like Tom to pat his head and say, "Good old scout, aren't you? Aren't you, Max? Good old scout, aren't you?" Enough to drive you crazy, when you're dying.

She lay with her eyes closed, and thought about dogs, and then about cats. People don't make such exorbitant demands upon cats, she thought. Nobody expects them to grin and pant and wag their tails and be overjoyed every time anyone speaks to them. No . . . People feel rather flattered if they can make a cat purr.

Birds . . . she thought. Why should everyone think that a skylark was so full of rapture? I think birds are frightfully fussy and worried. People say 'nervous as a cat.' I think 'nervous as a bird' would be much better. When you think of birds, hopping around, and chirping, and looking for food all the time . . . They push each other, too. I've seen them. They're rude, birds are.

There was a knock at the door, and she began to cry.

"Come in!" she called, drying her eyes roughly on the sheet.

It was David. He stood in the doorway, slight, too slight, in slacks and a blue shirt, and he was not smiling.

"I hear you're not feeling so fine," he said. "What's the trouble?"

"I'm tired, that's all," said Lucia.

"Well, I hadn't noticed you'd been doing such a heck of a lot lately," he said.

"Everyone gets tired, sometimes," said Lucia, nettled by this tone. "And, after all, I'm not fifteen, David."

"You look funny," he said. "I think we'd better get a doctor."

"No!" said Lucia. "I'm not going to have a doctor. All I need is a little rest."

"Well, I think you look funny," said David.

She fought against her anger; she reasoned with herself. It's always like this, she thought. Even Tom is sort of furious if I get sick. What have you been *doing* with yourself, to get a cold like this?

"I'll be all right, David, after a little rest," she said.

"Well . . ." said David, "I don't want to bother you, but there's one thing I'd like to ask you. What's happened to our car?"

"It's in the garage by the station."

"Well, I hope it is," said David.

"I *know* it is," said Lucia.

"Well, I hope so," said David.

Lucia closed her eyes, so that she need not see his irritating face.

"Mother?" he said, and when she did not answer: "*Mother?*" he said, in a different tone, in a panic.

"Oh, what *is* it, David?"

"Well, when you closed your eyes . . . I thought maybe you felt faint, or something."

She remembered him, when he was a little boy, shaking her by the shoulder, waking her out of a sound sleep, crying "Mother!" in that same tone. "What *is* it, David?" she had asked.

She remembered how he had looked, thin and wiry in his striped pajamas, his black hair ruffled. "I thought you were dead," he had said.

"I'm sorry I worried you, dear," she said. "Don't worry any more. I'll just rest for a while, and then I'll be perfectly all right."

She smiled at him, and his face relaxed.

"Okay!" he said. "Want anything from the village, Mother? Any medicine, or anything?"

"No, thank you, dear. But ask Sibyl what she wants."

It's going to be dreadful for David, she thought, when the story comes out. He wanted his mother to be not only conventional, and beyond measure respectable, but practically invisible. He had been disturbed even by her going out in the motorboat earlier than was the custom for mothers. How would it be when he learned what she was doing with the boat? And if he learned about Donnelly?

He had gone out of the room now, reassured about her health, but he left her miserably agitated, all the vague calmness gone. Now Bee will come, she thought. Bee was frightened yesterday. I know how she felt. When I was seventeen, if my mother had gone driving off with a strange man, leaving a guest she'd invited to tea, coming back so much later, and smelling of whisky . . . I'd have thought it was the end of the world. And I didn't explain anything to her.

Explain? *Explain?* But did I really do that? Did I help to put Nagle into that chest?

Oh, the chest is the worst! Far the worst. I drove the car, and I never even thought about the chest. He was there, in the chest, and I wasn't even sorry for him. Suppose he wasn't really dead? O God!

Sweat came out on her forehead. How do I know he was dead—when we put him—?

There was a knock at the door.

"May I come in, m'dear?"

"Oh, come in, Father!"

"Resting, eh?"

"Yes, I am, Father."

"Very good idea. Keeping house, in times like these—great strain. You need a rest, now and then."

"Well . . ."

"There's one thing, m'dear," he said, standing beside the bed. "I don't want to disturb your rest, but I dare say you can solve the mystery with one word."

"What mystery, Father?"

"Thing is," he said, lowering his voice, "I had a bottle of Scotch, in the sideboard. Hadn't even opened it. Well, dashed if it hasn't disappeared!"

"You've got another bottle, haven't you, Father?"

"Oh, yes. Yes. Plenty. But that's not the point, m'dear.

I put that bottle in the sideboard myself, day before yesterday. And it's gone. I don't like to ask Sibyl about it. Colored people are sensitive—and you can't blame them. Shouldn't like her to imagine I was accusing her."

"She wouldn't think that, Father. She knows how we feel about her."

But Sibyl did take his whisky! she thought, remembering. And I drank out of the bottle. And Nagle . . .

"It occurred to me . . ." he said. "D'you think Bee might have offered drinks to some of her friends?"

"She'd never *touch* your whisky without asking you, Father. And she doesn't drink whisky. Only a little glass of sherry, once in a great while. Bee isn't like that, Father."

"No, no. Naturally. Don't worry. Rest. Enjoy yourself. Don't worry about anything."

He laid his hand on her forehead.

"Headache?" he asked. "Any aches or pains, m'dear? The great thing is, if there's anything starting, to nip it in the bud."

She looked up at him, into his steady blue eyes that had never looked at her except with affection and trust, and tears rose in her own.

"I'm—just tired . . ." she said, very unsteadily.

"Come, come!" he said, in alarm. "That's not like you, m'dear. Nerves . . ."

She forced a smile; she could feel how stiff and forced a smile it was, but it satisfied him.

"That's better!" he said. "I'm going to write to Tom today. Going to tell him how you keep the flag flying, eh?"

When he had gone, she cried . . . She wanted to cry wildly and violently, but only a few slow tears ran down her face. Why doesn't Bee come? she thought. I want Bee to come.

She was asleep when Sibyl brought her lunch tray.

"Is Miss Bee home?" she asked.

"Yes, ma'am. Went down to the village with Master David, and they came back in the car."

"Sibyl . . . Haven't you heard anything?"

"They brought back an evening paper, ma'am. It's in that."

"What is it? Did they get him?"

"I'll bring you the paper, ma'am, soon as they start their lunch."

"Tell me."

"I'll bring you the paper, ma'am."

She waited, waited, waited, not even looking at the tray.

"Can't you eat anything, ma'am?"

"No. Let me see, Sibyl."

SLAYER CONFESSES UNSUSPECTED CRIME

QUESTIONED IN DARBY CASE, SUSPECT ADMITS FEUD MURDER

Early this morning, the Horton County police got not only a full account of the accidental slaying of Ted Darby on the 17th, but also the surprise confession of a murder wholly unsuspected by them.

At 3 A.M. a police car picked up Martin Donnelly, 42, who gave his residence as the Hotel De Vrees, New York City, and took him to headquarters for questioning in regard to the Darbv case.

DARBY DEATH ACCIDENTAL

In a statement to press representatives, Lieutenant Levy, of the Horton County police said that Donnelly's account of

Darby's death tallied with medical reports and other factors. The two men had, according to Donnelly's account, engaged in a quarrel, on the private pier of one of the Glendale Beach palatial estates, which Donnelly was unable to identify. In the course of the quarrel, Donnelly stated that he had pushed Darby off the pier, and had then gone back to his car, in which he had slept until morning.

Alarmed then by Darby's continued absence, Donnelly stated that he returned to the pier, where he found Darby's body impaled on an anchor in a motorboat. He ran the boat over to Simm's Island, four miles or so offshore, and concealed the body in a marsh.

Confession a Surprise

"We were wholly unprepared," Lieutenant Levy told press representatives, "for the confession which followed. Donnelly stated, voluntarily, that on the previous day he had strangled and killed Anton Karl Nagle, 57, believed by New York police to have been an associate of Donnelly's in black market activities.

Following Donnelly's directions, police found Nagle's body in a lake . . .

"Sibyl!" cried Lucia.

But Sibyl had gone, and she was alone.

Martin, you fool! You wicked, wicked fool! You can't get out of this. And you don't want to. You wanted to be arrested. You wanted to confess. You want to die—in the electric chair.

Well, I won't let you. I'll tell Lieutenant Levy the truth about Ted Darby.

That won't do any good. Ted Darby doesn't matter now. It's Nagle. He did that for me. Martin, you fool! You fool, to choose that dreadful death. You didn't trust me. You thought I'd give you away. Again.

I've got to talk to him. I've got to see him. And I never can. Never, never again. But it can't—

"Lieutenant Levy is here, ma'am," said Sibyl. "Shall I bring him up?"

"No, no! He can't come up here. No. Ask him to wait. I'll be down in a moment. No . . . Ask my father to come here, please."

"Mr. Harper's stepped out, ma'am."

This is too much. This is too much, Lucia thought. She got up, and tried to dress in haste, but her hands trembled so, her heart beat so fast. What dress? she thought, opening the closet door.

She took down the brown dress, and hung it up again. She took down a clean pink cotton dress, and that was not right. O God, I've got to hurry! What dress? She picked out two others, and laid them on a chair, and they were not right. O God, what shall I do? I've got to find the right dress . . .

There was a gray flannel skirt in the closet, with the hem half unripped. That was the right thing. With shaking hands she opened her preposterous sewing basket, a jumble of thread, darning silk, shoulder pads, bits of ribbon. She threaded a big darning needle with gray silk, and stitched up the hem, so badly that it was in puckers. She put on the skirt, and a white blouse, and forgetting to glance in the mirror, she went out of the room and down the stairs. She thought she heard Mrs. Lloyd's voice, but that was impossible.

She stopped in the hall outside the sitting room, and it was Mrs. Lloyd in there, sitting on the edge of a chair. She was stylish today, in a high black hat from which a cyclamen veil floated, and she was just drawing off a cyclamen glove. But Lieutenant Levy was not there.

He's in the dining room, Lucia thought, and was moving away when Bee called to her.

"Mother!"

"I'm sorry . . ." Lucia said. "I'm sorry, but I've got to see Lieutenant Levy."

"He's gone, Mother. Mother, Mrs. Lloyd is here."

"I know. But——"

Bee crossed the room and took her mother's hand.

"Come and sit down, Mother."

It was inhuman of Bee to ask her to sit down and talk to Mrs. Lloyd. She hung back, like a rebellious child, but Bee drew her forward.

"I'm afraid *I* drove Lieutenant Levy away," said Mrs. Lloyd.

"Oh, no!" said Bee. "He said it wasn't anything important. He just stopped by, to tell Mother that the Darby case was closed."

"I've been to a meeting of the hospital committee," Mrs. Lloyd said, "and everyone was talking about this case. The Donnelly man was absolutely desperate. He fought off the police like a tiger, for hours, and they had to shoot him in the leg before he'd give in. Mrs. Ewing heard the shots."

"I'm afraid Mrs. Ewing's mistaken," said Bee. "Mr. Donnelly didn't even try to get away."

"But these gunmen always seem to defy the police, don't they?"

"Mr. Donnelly isn't a gunman," said Bee. "You see, we know him."

"You *know* him?" said Mrs. Lloyd, fascinated.

"Yes. And we liked him, Grandpa, and David and me, and Mother . . ."

"Then weren't you appalled, when you found out what he'd done?"

"No," Bee said, rising. She sat down on the arm of the sofa beside Lucia, and laid her hand on her mother's shoulder. "We're just terribly sorry."

Her hand lay heavy on her mother's shoulder.

"He had lots of nice qualities," she said. "Only, the war makes people do—queer, horrible things." Her voice was a little unsteady now. "Especially middle-aged people."

"Oh, do you think so?" Mrs. Lloyd asked, a little surprised.

"Yes!" Bee said, vehemently. "It's psychological. Middle-aged people feel—sort of left out. As if everything was finished for them. They get a sort of craving for adventure . . ."

It was not Donnelly she was defending; it was her mother. She had tried to understand Lucia's bewildering and frightening behavior; she was trying now to present it as the foolish, but pitiable, last fling of a middle-aged woman. Lucia glanced up at her, and their eyes met.

"Mother," Bee said. "I'm sorry you felt so tired, but I thought I wouldn't bother you."

She had forgotten Mrs. Lloyd, so important in her scheme of life. All she wanted now was, that Lucia should know she understood, that she loved her.

"I'll look after the housekeeping for a while," she said. "And you can take things easy, Mother."

Be easy . . .

"Excuse me, ladies!" said Mr. Harper. "But the young fellow from the gas company wants to see the contract, Lucia."

"What contract, Father?"

"He says the owner of the house has a contract for maintenance. He must have left it with you, m'dear."

"I don't remember seeing it, Father."

"Well . . ." he said, indulgent and resigned, "if you can't find the contract, m'dear, we'll have to pay, and pay through the nose, for these repairs to the icebox." He smiled at Mrs. Lloyd. "I'm afraid you ladies don't take contracts very seriously," he said.

"I'm frightful about losing things," said Mrs. Lloyd.

This is my life, Lucia thought. The things I dreaded aren't going to happen, the shame, the disgrace. I don't know whether Lieutenant Levy believes Martin's story about Ted Darby, but anyhow he's going to accept it. Nothing's going to happen to me.

This is my life, going on just the same. I haven't hurt the children, or Tom, or Father. I haven't shocked people like Mrs. Lloyd. The man is here to fix the icebox, at last. This is how I'll go on.

And all that had happened to her would be, must be, pushed down, out of sight; the details of daily living would come like falling leaves to cover it. I don't really know what's happened to me, she thought, in wonder. I haven't taken time to think about it.

Maybe I never will. Or maybe, when I'm old, and have plenty of time and quiet . . .

Sibyl came in, with tea and cinnamon toast. The butter on the toast was margarine, colored yellow; the cinnamon was artificial. Lucia had read the label on the little tin with an unreasonable interest; she remembered some of it now. Imitation cinnamon. Cinnamic aldehyde. Eugenol. Oil of cassia, quite a lot of other things, too.

But nobody knows the difference, she thought. Only Sibyl and me.